Another Newcomer to Spooksville

The day the howling ghost kidnapped Cindy Makey's kid brother, Neil, was rotten from the start. But Cindy had begun to expect bad times ever since her family moved to Springville, or Spooksville, as all the kids in town called it. At first—even though she disliked the place—Cindy didn't believe half the stories she heard about it. But after the ghost came out of the lighthouse and grabbed Neil, she was ready to believe anything.

Books by Christopher Pike

Spooksville #1: The Secret Path
Spooksville #2: The Howling Ghost

Available from MINSTREL Books

CHRISTOPHER PIKE

SPOOKSVILLE #2 ™

THE HOWLING GHOST

A MINSTREL® BOOK

Published by POCKET BOOKS
New York   London   Toronto   Sydney   Tokyo   Singapore

This book is a work of fiction. Names, characters, places and incidents are products of the author's imagination or are used fictitiously. Any resemblance to actual events or locales or persons, living or dead, is entirely coincidental.

A MINSTREL PAPERBACK *Original*

 A Minstrel Book published by
POCKET BOOKS, a division of Simon & Schuster Inc.
1230 Avenue of the Americas, New York, NY 10020

ISBN: 0-671-53726-1

First Minstrel Books printing November 1995

10 9 8 7 6 5 4 3 2 1

A MINSTREL BOOK and colophon are registered trademarks of Simon & Schuster Inc.

Front cover illustration Lee MacLeod

Printed in the U.S.A.

SPOOKSVILLE™ #2

THE HOWLING GHOST

The day the howling ghost kidnapped Cindy Makey's kid brother, Neil, was rotten from the start. Cindy began to expect bad times ever since her family moved to Springville, or Spooksville, as the kids in town called it. At first—even though she disliked the place—Cindy didn't believe half the stories she heard about it. But after the ghost came out of the lighthouse and grabbed Neil, she was ready to believe anything.

"Can I walk on the jetty?" Neil asked as they

reached the end of the beach, where the rocky jetty led out to the lighthouse.

"I don't think so," Cindy replied, stuffing her hands in her pockets. "It's getting late and cold."

"Please?" Neil pleaded, sounding like the five-year-old he was. "I'll be careful."

Cindy smiled at her brother. "You don't know what the word means."

Neil frowned. "Which word?"

"Careful, dummy." Cindy stared at the churning ocean water. The waves weren't high, but the way they smashed against the large boulders of the jetty made her uneasy. It was as if the surf were trying to tear down the structure. And the tall lighthouse, standing dark and silent at the end of the jetty, also made her nervous. It had ever since she moved to Springville two months ago. The lighthouse just looked, well, kind of spooky.

"Pretty please?" Neil asked again.

Cindy sighed. "All right. But stay in the middle, and watch where you put your feet. I don't want you falling in."

Neil leaped in the air. "Cool! Do you want to come?"

Cindy turned away. "No. I'll sit here and watch.

But if a shark comes out of the water and carries you out to sea, I'm not going in after you."

Neil stopped bouncing. "Do sharks eat boys?"

"Only when there are no girls to eat." Seeing Neil's confused expression, Cindy laughed and sat down on a large rock. "That was a joke. Go, quick, have your walk on the jetty. Then let's get home. It'll be dark in a few minutes."

"OK," he said, dancing away, talking to himself. "Watch out for falling feet and girl sharks."

"Just be careful," Cindy said, so softly she was sure Neil didn't hear. She wondered why the dread she felt about the town hadn't touched her brother. Since their mother had moved them back to their father's old house eight weeks ago, Neil had been as happy as one of the smiling clams he occasionally found on the beach.

But Cindy knew the town wasn't safe. In Springville the nights were just a little too dark, the moon a little too big. Sometimes in the middle of the night she heard strange sounds: leathery wings beating far overhead, muted cries echoing from under the ground. Maybe she imagined these things—she wasn't sure. She just wished her father were still alive to go with them on their walks. Actually, she just wished he were alive. She missed him more than she knew how to say.

Still, she kept going for walks late in the evening. Particularly by the ocean. It seemed to draw her. Even the spooky lighthouse called to her.

Watching Neil scale the first of the large boulders, Cindy began to sing a song her father had taught her. Actually, it was more of an old poem that she chanted. The words were not pleasant. But for some strange reason they came back to Cindy right then.

> The ocean is a lady,
> She is kind to all.
> But if you forget her dark moods.
> Her cold waves, those watery walls.
> Then you are bound to fall.
> Into a cold grave.
> Where the fish will have you for food.
>
> The ocean is a princess.
> She is always fair.
> But if you dive too deep.
> Into the abyss, the octopus's lair.
> Then you are bound to despair.
> In a cold grave.
> Where the sharks will have you for meat.

4

"My father never was much of a poet," Cindy muttered when she finished the piece. Of course, she knew he hadn't made it up. Someone had taught it to him. She just didn't know who. Maybe *his* mother or father, who had lived in Springville when her father was five.

Cindy wondered if he had ever walked out to the lighthouse.

Without warning, the top of the lighthouse began to glow right then.

"Oh no," Cindy muttered as she got to her feet. Everyone knew the lighthouse was deserted. A pillar of spider webs and dust. Light had not shone from its windows since she'd moved to Springville. Her mother said it hadn't been turned on in decades.

Yet as she watched, a powerful beam of white light stabbed out from the top of the lighthouse. It was turned toward the sea. It raked over the water like an energy beam fired from an alien ship. The surface of the water churned harder beneath its glare, as if it were boiling. Steam appeared to rise up from the cold water. For a moment she thought she saw something just under the surface. A ruined ship, maybe, wrecked on a sharp reef that grew over it with the passing years.

Then the light snapped toward the shore, spinning halfway around. It focused on the jetty. Still moving, still searching.

Cindy watched in horror as it crept toward her brother.

He was already partway down the jetty, his eyes focused on his feet.

"Neil!" she screamed.

He looked up just as the light fell on him. It was as if something physical had grabbed him. For a few seconds his short brown hair stood straight up. Then his feet lifted off the boulder he was standing on. The light was so bright it was blinding. But Cindy got the impression that two ugly hands had emerged from the light to take hold of him. As a second scream rose in her throat, she thought she saw the hands tighten their grip.

"Get away, Neil!" she cried.

Cindy was running toward her brother. But the light was faster than she was. Before she even reached the jetty, Neil was yanked completely into the air. For several seconds he floated above the rocks and surf, an evil wind tugging at his hair, terror in his eyes.

"Neil!" Cindy kept screaming, leaping from boulder to boulder, not caring where her feet landed. But that was her undoing. She was almost to her brother, within arm's reach, when her shoes hit a piece of wet seaweed. She slipped and went down hard. Pain flared in her right leg. She had scraped the skin off her knee.

"Cindy!" her brother finally called. But the word sounded strange, the cry of a lost soul falling into a deep well. As Cindy watched, her brother was yanked out over the water, away from the jetty. He was held suspended, as the waves crashed beneath his feet and the wind howled.

Yet this was not a natural wind. It howled as if alive. Or else it shouted as if it hungered for those still living. The sound seemed to come from the beam of light itself. There was a note of sick humor in the sound. A wicked chuckle. It had her brother. It had what it wanted.

"Neil," Cindy whispered, in despair.

He tried to speak to her, perhaps to say her name again.

But no words came out.

The beam of light suddenly moved.

It jerked her brother farther out over the sea. Far out over the rough surf. For a few seconds Cindy could still see him, a struggling shadow in the glare of the cold light. But then the beam swept upward, toward the sky. And went out.

Just like that, the light vanished.
Taking her brother with it.
"Neil!" Cindy cried.
But the wind continued to howl.
And her cry was lost over the cruel sea.
No one heard her. No one came to help.

2

Two days after Cindy Makey's brother was kidnapped by the howling ghost, Adam Freeman and Sally Wilcox were having breakfast with their friend Watch. Breakfast was doughnuts and milk at the local bakery. Of course, Sally was having coffee instead of milk because, as she said, the caffeine helped steady her nerves.

"What's wrong with your nerves?" Adam asked, munching on a jelly doughnut.

"If you had lived here as long as me, you wouldn't have to ask," Sally replied, sipping her coffee. She nodded to his doughnut. "It's better to eat ones that don't have stuff inside."

"Why?" Adam asked.

"You never know what that *stuff* might be," Sally said.

"It's just a jelly doughnut," Adam protested, although he did stop eating it.

Sally spoke gravely. "Yeah, but where did the jelly come from? Have you been in the back room? Have you studied the supplies? You can make jelly out of raspberries and strawberries, or a respectable facsimile from scrambled brains."

Adam set his doughnut down. "I really don't think so."

"It's not always wise to think too much in this town," Sally said. "Sometimes you've got to trust your gut feelings." She leaned over and sniffed the doughnut. "Or your nose. It smells all right to me, Adam. Go ahead, have another bite."

Adam sipped his milk. "I've had enough."

"Can I finish it?" Watch asked. "I'm not picky."

"Sure," Adam said, pushing the doughnut over. "What were we talking about a few seconds ago? I forgot."

"Alien abductions," Watch said, taking a bite out of

the doughnut and licking the jelly as it oozed over his fingers. "They're happening all over. Ships from other planets come down and grab people and take them into orbit for physical examinations. I'm surprised one of us hasn't been abducted yet. I imagine we would make interesting specimens."

"I don't believe in flying saucers," Adam said.

Sally snorted. "Yeah. Just like you didn't believe in witches a month ago."

"Have you ever seen a flying saucer?" Adam asked even though he knew what Sally's answer would be.

"Of course," she said. "Just before you got here I saw one come down up at the reservoir. Old Man Farmer was out on his boat fishing and—"

"Wait a second," Adam interrupted. "I thought you said there were no fish in the reservoir? That they had all thrown themselves on the shore because they couldn't bear to live there."

"I said he was fishing," Sally explained. "I didn't say he was catching any fish. Anyway, this ship came down and hovered over him and emitted this high vibration. Before you knew it Farmer's face got really long and his eyes bulged out of his head. Ten seconds of this and he looked like an alien."

"Then what?" Adam asked.

Sally shrugged nonchalantly. "The ship left and he continued fishing. I think he caught something that day, too. But I don't know if it was edible."

"But did Mr. Farmer continue to look like an alien?" Adam asked, exasperated.

"It was not a lasting operation," Sally said.

"But his chin is still kind of pointed," Watch added.

Adam shook his head. "I don't believe any of this."

"Why don't you take a peek in the back," Sally said. "Old Man Farmer works here. He probably baked that doughnut you just ate."

As often was the case when Adam was with his friends, he had to struggle to keep up. If he hadn't almost been thrown in a boiling vat on the Secret Path, he would have refused to believe this new story. But nowadays he always left the door to his mind open, in case what they were talking about might be true.

"What I want to know," Adam said, "is why Spooksville is so spooky? What is it about this place that makes it different from other towns?"

Watch nodded. "That's the big question. I've been trying to figure out the answer since I moved here. But I can tell you one thing, Bum knows the truth. I think Ann Templeton does, too."

"But Bum won't tell?" Adam asked.

"Nope," Watch said. "He said I have to find the answer for myself. And that I will probably disappear from the face of the earth before I do." He paused. "You might want to talk to Ann Templeton about it sometime. I hear you guys are friends."

"Who told you that?" Adam asked.

Watch pointed at Sally. "She did."

"What I said was that he was in love with the witch," Sally explained. "I didn't say they were friends."

"I don't love her," Adam snapped.

"Well, you certainly don't love me," Sally snapped back.

Adam scratched his head. "How did we go from what makes Spooksville scary to my personal life."

"What personal life?" Sally asked, getting annoyed. "You don't have a personal life. You don't even have a girlfriend."

"I'm twelve years old," Adam said. "I'm not required to have a girlfriend."

"That's right," Sally said. "Wait till you're eighteen. Let your whole life pass you by. Throw away your finest years. I don't care. I live in the present moment. That's the only way to live in this town. Because tomorrow you might be dead. Or worse."

Watch patted Sally on the back. "I think you need another doughnut."

Sally grumbled, still looking at Adam. "Doughnuts cannot cure all my problems." Nevertheless, she took a bite out of the chocolate one Watch set in front of her. A smile touched her lips. "Ah, sugar and chocolate. Better than love. They're always there for you."

Adam looked away and muttered, "You should carry a box of chocolates wherever you go."

"I heard that," Sally said, still munching her doughnut, which may have had a little jelly in the center of it, too. Casually, she reached behind her and lifted a newspaper off the next table. She studied the news for a few seconds. "Oh no," she moaned.

"What is it?" Adam asked.

"A five-year-old boy disappeared off the jetty, down by the lighthouse," Sally said.

"Didn't you know?" Watch asked. "It was in yesterday's paper. A wave came up and carried him off. The police say he must have drowned."

"Drowned?" Sally repeated, pointing to the article. "His sister was with him at the time, and she says a ghost came out of the lighthouse and grabbed the kid."

Watch shrugged. "Either way the kid's a goner."

"Have they found his body?" Adam asked, feeling

sick. He didn't know what it would be like to drown, but imagined it would be like smothering.

"No," Sally said, reading the article. "The police say the tide must have carried the boy out. The idiots."

"But that sounds logical," Adam said, although he was sure Sally would yell at him for saying it. Sally huffed and tossed the paper aside.

"Don't you see?" she asked. "They haven't found a body because he didn't drown. The kid's sister is telling the truth. A ghost swiped the kid. Watch, why don't you explain to Adam that these things happen. This is reality."

Watch was not interested. "Like I said, it doesn't matter whether it was a ghost or a wave. The kid's dead by now."

Sally was annoyed. "He's just another Spooksville statistic to you? How can you be so cold? What if he's alive?"

Watch blinked at her. "That would be nice."

"No!" Sally yelled. "What if he's alive and needs to be rescued? We're the only ones who can do it."

"Really?" Watch asked.

"Of course," Sally said. "I believe this girl. I believe in ghosts."

"I don't," Adam said.

Sally glared. "You're just afraid of them. That's why you're willing to leave this poor young boy to a life of torment. Really, Adam, I'm disappointed in you."

Adam could feel himself getting a headache. "I have nothing against this kid. But if the police couldn't find him, I don't think we can."

Sally stood up. "Great. Give up without trying. Next time a witch or an alien kidnaps you, I'll just order a cup of coffee and a jelly doughnut and tell whoever's around that Adam was a nice guy and I really cared for him but if he's gone he's gone and there's no sense searching for him because I can't be bothered." She paused to catch her breath. "Well?"

"Well, what?" Adam asked.

Sally put her hands on her hips. "Are you going to help me or not?"

Adam glanced at Watch, who had picked up the paper and was reading the article. "Are we helping her or not?" Adam asked his friend.

Watch glanced at his watches, all four of them, two on each arm. "It's not as if we're doing anything this afternoon." He added, "I know Cindy Makey. She's cute."

Adam turned back to Sally. "We'll help you."

Sally fumed as she turned away. "You guys are so altruistic."

Adam glanced at Watch as he stood up, ready to follow Sally. "What does *altruistic* mean?" he whispered to Watch.

"Let's just say the word does not apply to us," Watch whispered back.

3

Cindy was sitting outside her house, slowly rocking on a wooden porch swing. Adam felt a pang in his chest—her face was so sad. She didn't even hear them approach. She seemed absorbed in her own private world. A world where her little brother was no longer there. In that moment Adam would have given anything to get the missing kid back.

But then Adam remembered what Watch had said. Either way it was probably hopeless.

"Hello," Sally said as they stepped onto the girl's porch. "Are you Cindy Makey?"

Watch was right, she was pretty. Her hair was long and blond; it reached almost to her waist. Her eyes were wide and deep blue. They reminded Adam of the sky just before the sun came up. Yet her eyes were also red. She had been crying just before they arrived.

"Yes," Cindy said softly.

Sally stepped forward and offered her hand. "Hi, I'm Sally Wilcox and this is Adam Freeman and Watch. We may not look like much, but we're intelligent and resourceful individuals. Best of all, we've been through pretty weird stuff. We believe in almost everything, including your ghost." Sally paused to catch her breath. "We're here to help you get your brother back."

Cindy took a moment to absorb everything Sally had just said. She gestured to another two-person swing.

"Do you want to sit down?" she said quietly. "Are you thirsty? Would you like some lemonade?"

"We never take refreshment until the job is done," Sally said, sitting down.

"I'd like some lemonade," Adam said, sitting beside Sally.

"Adam," Sally scolded. "We're here to help Cindy, not take from her."

Adam shrugged. "But I'm thirsty."

"So am I," Watch added. "Do you have any Coke?"

Cindy stood. "We have Coke and lemonade. I'll be back in a second. Are you sure you don't want anything, Sally?"

Sally considered. "Well, now that you mention it. Do you have any ginger ale? I like Canada Dry best, in the green cans. Chilled but not too cold."

Cindy nodded. "I'll see what we have."

Cindy disappeared inside the house. Adam spoke to Watch, who continued to stand. He was staring in the direction of the ocean.

"What are you looking at?" Adam asked.

Watch pointed. "The lighthouse. You can see it from here."

Watch was right. Around the corner of the house, the lighthouse was just visible, a tall pillar of white plaster. At this first sight of the structure, Adam shuddered, although he wasn't sure why. He had never seen a lighthouse before he saw this one. It was hard for him to tell a normal one from a haunted one. It was only a quarter of a mile away.

"It's tall," was all Adam could think of to say.

"It's old," Watch said, finally sitting down. "It was built before there was electricity. From what I heard, they used to burn oil in lamps in the top and shine the light over the sea to warn ships away from the rocks."

"I heard they used to burn people," Sally said.

"People don't burn that well," Watch replied matter-of-factly. "Bum once told me it was the Spaniards who built the lighthouse, that it was the first one constructed in America. But it's hard to imagine it's that old."

"But later electricity was installed?" Adam asked.

"Sure," Watch said. "The waters around Spooksville are treacherous. Even modern ships have to be careful. Yet the lighthouse was closed down before I was born. I'm not sure why. Nowadays, ships don't get near this place. The last boat that did go by was a transport ship from Japan. It had hundreds of Toyotas on board. It sunk out by the jetty. For a while you could go down to the beach and pick out any color Camry or Corolla that you wanted. They washed ashore for months."

"They all smelled a little fishy," Sally said.

"But you couldn't argue with the price," Watch added.

"I'd never go out with a guy who had fish on his backseat," Sally said.

"There must've been a reason the lighthouse was closed down," Adam said.

"Probably because it was haunted," Sally said. "That's the most logical reason."

"But why did it become haunted?" Adam asked. "That's what I want to know."

A look of wonder crossed Sally's face. "Why, Adam, you're beginning to sound like you were born here. Congratulations—from now on I won't have to yell at you half as much."

"I don't know why you yell at me at all," Adam said. He glanced in the direction of where Cindy had disappeared. "She looks so sad."

Watch nodded. "Like a flower that's been stomped."

"A rose that's been crushed," Adam agreed, feeling in a poetic mood.

"Wait a second," Sally complained. "You guys aren't falling in love with her, are you?"

"Love is an emotion I only know about from textbooks," Watch said.

"I just met her," Adam said. "I don't even know her."

"But as soon as you met me you liked me, didn't you?" Sally asked.

Adam shrugged. "I suppose."

Sally suddenly looked worried, and a little annoyed. "Just don't go flirting with her while I'm around."

"We'll wait and do it behind your back," Watch said tactfully.

Cindy returned a minute later. She had two tall glasses of Coke, with ice, and one lemonade. Offering a Coke to Sally, Cindy apologized that there was no ginger ale.

"I suppose I could use the caffeine," Sally said, sniffing her drink before sipping it.

Adam gulped down his lemonade. "Ah," he said between gulps. "There's nothing like lemonade on a hot day."

"It was cold a couple days ago," Cindy remarked sadly, sitting down.

Adam set his drink down and spoke gently. "It was cold when your brother disappeared?"

Cindy nodded. "Yes. There was a strong wind—it whipped across the water, stirring up the waves." She stopped to shake her head. "We shouldn't have been walking by the jetty."

"What time of day was it?" Sally asked seriously.

"Sunset," Cindy said. "But you couldn't see the sun because of the gray clouds."

"Were both of you walking on the jetty?" Adam asked.

"No," Cindy said. "Neil was alone. I mean, I could see him and everything. I was sitting on a boulder. He had walked alone on the jetty many times before. He was always careful to watch where he stepped.

He never walked out too far. It was just that this time . . ." Cindy's voice trailed off and she lowered her head. It seemed, for a moment, that she was going to cry, but she didn't. She also didn't finish her sentence.

"It was just that this time a ghost grabbed him?" Sally said.

Cindy took a breath. "I think so."

"But you're not sure?" Adam asked gently.

Cindy shook her head. "It happened so fast. Something came and took him. I don't know what it was."

"Are you sure he didn't just fall into the water?" Watch asked.

Cindy raised her head. "He didn't fall in the water. He didn't drown. I told the police that. I told my mother—but none of them believe me." She paused and stared at each of them. "Do you believe me?"

"We told you we did," Sally said, eyeing Watch to be quiet. "We just want to be sure of the facts. When you're dealing with a ghost, you have to be careful. Can you describe this ghost to us?"

"Neil was walking along the jetty when a beam of light shot out from the top of the lighthouse. It was a blinding light and seemed to be searching for Neil. When it caught up to him, old hands came out of the light and grabbed him. I know he was lifted into the air before the light went off and he vanished. I saw him floating above the water, above the rocks."

"This is what you told the police?" Adam asked.

"Yes," Cindy said. "This is exactly what happened."

"Did the police examine the lighthouse?" Watch asked.

"I don't know," Cindy said. "I told them to, but they just said the lighthouse was all boarded up, that no light could have come from it. After hearing my story, they were convinced my brother had fallen in the water and been swept out to sea. They thought I was hallucinating because I was in shock."

"A typical authoritarian response," Sally said.

"There was one other thing," Cindy said. "When the hands came out of the light and grabbed Neil, the wind howled. But it was a weird sound. It was like some evil monster laughing."

"Was it a female monster or a male monster?" Adam asked.

"That's a very weird question," Sally remarked.

"I don't know," Watch disagreed. "Personally, I'd rather deal with a male monster any day."

"My feeling exactly," Adam muttered.

Cindy was thoughtful. "I think it was a female monster."

"Let's not call it a monster," Sally interrupted. "It sounds more like a ghost." She touched Cindy on the knee. "We're going to get your brother back, no matter what."

"We're going to *try* to get him back," Adam corrected.

"As long as we don't have to risk our own lives," Watch added.

Cindy's lower lip quivered, and her eyes were wet. "Thank you—all of you. You don't know what it means to me to have someone believe me. I know he's alive, I feel it in my heart." Cindy paused. "The only thing is: what do we do now?"

Adam stood up, and with more courage than he knew he had, said, "It's obvious. We break into the lighthouse."

The way to the lighthouse was hard. Not only was the lighthouse at the end of the jetty, but also the narrow wooden bridge that crossed from the piled boulders to the lighthouse itself was worn and cracked. Adam took one look at it and wished he'd brought his bathing suit. The bridge looked as if it would collapse the moment he stepped on it.

Fortunately, the ocean was calm. The waves brushing against the jetty were only a foot high. Adam believed if he fell in the water, he'd have no trouble getting out. But then Sally started on her gruesome history of Spooksville again.

"It was near here that Jaws lost his leg," Sally said as they stared down at the water that separated them from the lighthouse.

"Who?" Adam asked, with regret.

"David Green," Sally said. "He was the guy I told you about. He was out on his boogie board when a great white shark came by and bit off his right leg. In fact, I think it was almost at this exact spot."

"I thought you said he was close to shore when he was attacked," Adam said, glancing back the way they had come. Jumping from rock to rock to reach the end of the jetty had not been difficult, but they were nevertheless pretty far from the beach. Adam wouldn't like to be out on the jetty when the surf was up. The waves would crash right over them.

"I can't remember every detail," Sally replied. "All I know is if you go in this water, you will probably come out with pieces missing."

Adam turned to Watch. "The bridge looks as if it's about to fall. I don't know if we should risk it."

"The girls weigh less," Watch said. "We should send one of them across first to see how it holds up."

"Watch!" Sally yelled. "You miserable coward!"

"I was just making a logical suggestion," Watch said.

"I'll go first," Cindy said quietly. "If my brother's in the lighthouse, I should be the one to take the biggest risks."

Sally patted her on the back. "I wish I had a sister as devoted as you."

Adam stepped between them. "Wait a second. This isn't right. One of us guys should go first."

"Are you forgetting that there are only two of us *guys* here?" Watch asked.

"Why are you being such a coward?" Adam asked. "It's not like you."

Watch shrugged. "I don't want to hurt Cindy's feelings, but I think the chances that her brother is locked in the lighthouse are lousy. For that reason I don't want to lose a leg or an arm." He paused and glanced at Cindy, who had lowered her head at his words. "But if you all want to give it a try, I'll go first."

Watch took a step toward the rickety bridge. Adam stopped him.

"I'm lighter than you," Adam said. "I'll go first."

Watch glanced down at the blue water, which had begun to churn slightly since they arrived. "All right,"

Watch said. "If the bridge breaks, get out of the water as quick as you can."

Adam nodded and felt his heart pound in his chest. He was about to take his first step onto the bridge when a hand touched his arm. It was Cindy. Her face was creased with worry. For the second time that day he thought how beautiful her blue eyes were, how bright the sun shone in her blond hair.

"Be careful, Adam," Cindy whispered.

Adam smiled. "I'm used to danger. It doesn't faze me."

"Yeah," Sally said sarcastically. "Mr. Kansas City grew up wrestling great white sharks in his backyard swimming pool."

Adam ignored Sally and turned back to the bridge. It had handrails that were made of rope and looked every bit as old as the wooden planks beneath them. Carefully placing his weight on the first plank, Adam took a step above the water. He had to try hard not to glance down at the water. It looked awfully cold and deep. If he stared real hard he could imagine huge shapes just below the surface.

Adam took another step forward. The bridge creaked uneasily and sagged beneath him. He now had his entire weight on it. A third step forward caused the bridge to sink even more. It was only twenty feet from the end of the jetty to the pile of stones that supported the lighthouse, but at the rate he was going, he wouldn't reach it till next month. The thought came to him that perhaps if he hurried, the bridge wouldn't feel his weight as much. It was a brave idea, but a bit foolish.

Adam took off running across the bridge.

He was inches from the other side when it broke.

The bridge didn't just break in one spot. The whole thing collapsed. One second Adam was running for his life and the next he was swimming for it. He hit the water hard and went under. His timing was bad. He was sucking in a breath when he slipped under the surface. As a result he came up choking. He could hear the others yelling, but he couldn't answer them. Saltwater stung his eyes. He coughed hard and flayed with his arms. The water was freezing!

"Swim!" Sally cried. "A shark's coming!"

Adam almost had a heart attack right then. The day he moved to Spooksville, a tree had almost swallowed him. But in his mind getting eaten by a shark would be a thousand times worse. Frantically he spun around, trying to get his bearings. He didn't know if he was closer to the lighthouse or the jetty, and at the moment he really didn't care. He just wanted to get out of the water.

"I don't see any shark!" he heard Cindy yell.

"You don't see them till it's too late!" Sally yelled back. "Adam! Save yourself!"

Adam stopped choking long enough to look back at his friends. "Is there really a shark?" he gasped, treading water.

Watch shook his head. "I don't see one."

"Yeah, but you're almost blind," Adam said.

"I don't see one either," Cindy said.

"This is a big ocean and there are sharks in it somewhere," Sally said impatiently. "If you don't hurry and get out of the water, I'm sure you will see one soon enough."

"Oh brother," Adam grumbled, tired of Sally. He saw he was closer to the lighthouse than the jetty and decided to swim for it. A few seconds later he was out of the water and shivering beside the front door of the lighthouse. Now he knew why the police hadn't bothered to check out Cindy's story. What was left of the bridge smashed back and forth against the jetty as the surf played with the wooden planks. In a sense, he was trapped, unless he wanted to get back in the water and wait for Sally's next shark attack.

"Can you feel your legs?" Sally called across the distance.

"Yes," Adam called back. "They're still attached to my body, thank you."

"Try the door to the lighthouse," Watch said. "There might be a rope inside that you can throw to us."

The door—no surprise—was locked. Adam looked around for a large rock to break the handle. He doubted that the ghost inside would sue him for damaging his property.

But this was Spooksville. He probably should have thought more about what he was doing. But he was cold; his clothes were soaked. He just wanted to get inside, so he could dry off. Picking up a stone as big as his head, he brought it down hard on the doorknob. The knob broke off, and the door swung open.

It was dark inside. How clever of them to forget flashlights. Adam took several steps forward, once again feeling his heart pound. There was a musty smell; the place had been locked up a long time. His shoes left clear prints in the dust on the wooden floor. Water dripped from his clothes, smearing the dust. From the light that poured in through the door, he was able to see a spiral staircase that wound up to the top of the lighthouse. The very top was lost in shadows, and the stairway seemed to vanish into unnatural night.

33

"Hello," he called.

The word echoed back to him.

Hello. Hello. Hello.

Each repetition was heavier than the one before, more spooky.

Hollo. Hollo. Hollo.

Actually, it sounded as if a ghost were talking.

Ollo. Ollo. Ollo

But not a friendly ghost. Not one welcoming him.

Ogo. Ogo. Ogo.

Adam shivered as he listened to the sound.

Go. Go. Go.

There was a small storage room off to his left. Inside was a shovel, a wheelbarrel, several metal containers that smelled of kerosene, and a rope. Surprisingly, the rope was fairly new, in better shape than the other equipment. He hurried back outside and held it up for the others to see. Watch spoke for all of them with his next questions.

"Do you want to use it to get back here?" he asked. "Or do you want us to come over there?"

Cindy stepped forward. "I want to search the lighthouse," she said. "I have to."

Sally eyed the water uneasily. "If the rope breaks, we'll all end up in a shark's belly."

"Is there a good place to tie it on your side?" Watch called to Adam.

Adam glanced back at the winding stairway. He had at least a couple hundred feet of rope in his hands. It would reach, he decided. "Yeah," he said. "Do you have anything to tie it to on the jetty?"

Watch studied the boulders. "Sure," he said. "But we'll be dangling just above the waterline."

"I wonder how high a shark can reach out of the water?" Sally muttered.

Adam threw one end of the rope over to Watch, who wrapped it around a boulder. Before Watch tied his end off, Adam reentered the lighthouse and secured his end to the stairway. He knew it was ridiculous, but he thought he heard his *hello* still echoing. It was only a faint moan though.

Oooooo.

Adam went back outside. Watch had drawn the rope tight and tied it. It stretched only three feet above the water. "Who's going first?" Adam called.

Cindy grabbed hold of the rope. "I will." Then she paused. "What do I do?"

"Start with your back to the lighthouse," Watch explained. "Grab the rope tightly with your hands and pull yourself out slowly. When you're above the water, throw your feet around the rope, too. And don't fall off."

Cindy did what Watch instructed. Soon she was inching her way toward Adam. The ends of her blond hair brushed the tips of the small waves. Adam wanted to say something to encourage her, but couldn't think of anything—especially with Sally glaring at him.

Adam just didn't understand Sally. She had been the one who wanted to help Cindy in the first place. Just because he said a few nice things about Cindy was no reason for Sally to get so jealous. Adam didn't even know what there was to be jealous about. They were kids and weren't into relationships. He wasn't even sure what the word meant.

"Just a few more feet," Adam said finally when Cindy was almost across. When her feet were above the stones, he reached out and helped her off the rope. She stood beside him and caught her breath.

"That was scary," she said.

"How long have you lived in Spooksville?" he asked.

"Two months. How about you?"

"Two weeks. We moved because of my dad's job."

Cindy's face fell. "We moved because my dad died."

"Oh. I'm sorry."

"His family had a house here that we stay in for free." Cindy shrugged weakly. "We had nowhere else to go."

"You don't have any other brothers or sisters? Beside Neil?"

"No."

"Hey!" Sally called from across the water, her hand on the rope. "Stop talking and get ready to rescue me if I fall in."

"I can't wait to rescue you again," Adam called back.

Sally took longer to cross than Cindy. Actually, she complained so much the whole way it was amazing she had enough strength left to hold on to the rope. But finally she was standing beside them.

"I hope we're not in a hurry on the way back," Sally said.

Watch was over in a few moments. The rope was strong; it hardly even sagged under Watch's weight. As long as there were no great whites in the area, they decided, they should have a safe return trip.

As a group, they entered the lighthouse. The ground floor was basically empty. Except for the storage area, and a bunch of spider webs, there was only dust. The spiral stairway seemed to wait for them, daring them, if they had the nerve, to climb its many steps into darkness. Adam gestured above.

"I wish we had at least one flashlight," he said.

"When we left home we were just going for doughnuts," Watch said. He tested the metal steps with both his hands. "The stairway appears strong enough. I bet it leads up to a door of some kind."

"Why do you say that?" Sally asked.

"It's dark in here," Watch explained. "But the lighthouse windows are not boarded up. You can see that from the outside. There must be a floor of some kind above us that blocks us from the windows." He stepped onto the stairway. "I guess we'll see in a few minutes."

"Should we go up together?" Sally asked, glancing around nervously.

"You can stay here all by yourself," Adam said, following Watch onto the steps. "But you've seen enough horror films to know what happens when you're all alone in a dark place."

"I grew up in this town," Sally snapped. "I watch horror films to relax before I go to sleep." She put a foot onto the stairway. "I just hope these steps don't suddenly end."

"It would be a long fall," Watch agreed, taking the lead.

"I just hope my brother's up there," Cindy said quietly, walking a step behind Adam.

The hike up the stairs was very hard. They were panting within a few minutes. And the floor looked so far away so quickly; it made Adam dizzy to look down. Also, it was unnerving to climb into blackness. Occasionally a spider web would settle over their faces and make them jump. Adam wished he had a Bic lighter or something to see with. The higher they climbed, the darker it got, and the warmer. Adam was about to call for Watch to stop and rest when Watch shouted, "Ouch!" He was practically invisible in the dark.

"We've reached the top," Watch said, rubbing the top of his head.

"Is there a door?" Sally asked, crowding up between Adam and Cindy.

"I smashed my head against something—I hope it's a door," Watch said. "Stay cool, I'm about to pound it with my fist to try to open it."

Watch pounded on what sounded like a wooden door several times without success.

"You might want to use your head," Sally suggested. "You had better luck with it."

"Maybe there's a lock," Cindy said, slipping past Adam, who could hardly see her. Adam listened for a moment while Watch and Cindy ran their fingers over the wooden door above them. Then suddenly there was a click and a ray of light struck Adam's face. It was coming from outside, through the windows at the top of the lighthouse. Cindy and Watch had pushed open the trapdoor.

As a group, they climbed into the top of the lighthouse.

It was dusty as well, and there were cobwebs everywhere. The dust lay particularly thick on the huge metal mirror that curved behind the giant searchlight that stood in the center of the room. Watch drew his finger over the mirror, and Adam was surprised to see how shiny the metal was beneath the dust. The twin bulbs that formed the heart of the searchlight were not covered by glass; they bulged near the center of the mirror like two watchful eyes. Watch studied the searchlight for a moment, checking on the wires that led to it.

"This thing hasn't been turned on in years," he said finally.

Cindy was disturbed. "It came on two days ago."

"Are you sure the light came from here?" Adam asked.

"Positive," Cindy said.

Watch was doubtful. "These wires are worn. I don't

think they're capable of carrying an electrical current."

"I know what I saw," Cindy insisted. She scanned the rest of the room. "He must be here somewhere," she said softly, desperately.

Adam tried to make her feel better. "If a ghost did take your brother, it might have taken him somewhere else."

Cindy sighed. "So, you're saying he could be anywhere, which is the same as saying we're never going to find him."

"No," Adam said quickly. "I meant we've only begun to search. Let's look around some more."

There wasn't much to the room. Besides the searchlight, there was a plain wooden desk and chair, a simple cot, and a bathroom that looked as if it hadn't been used in years. The faucet in the sink didn't even work. When they tried it, a faint smell of gas came out instead of water.

But Sally did find something unusual on one side of the desk. Carved in the old wood, on opposite sides of a roughly shaped heart, were two words: *Mommy* and *Rick*. The words were probably carved by a child. Adam looked to Sally and Watch.

"Do you know who operated the lighthouse last?" Adam asked.

"I heard it was a bloodsucking sailor," Sally said.

Watch shook his head. "No. The bloodsucker was the guy who used to run the bait shop on the pier. Bum said the lighthouse was last run by a woman—an old woman."

"Is she dead now?" Cindy asked.

"Most old people in Spooksville are dead," Sally said.

Watch nodded. "This was at least thirty years ago. I'm sure the woman is dead."

"You have to be dead to be a ghost," Sally said, trying to encourage Cindy.

"What about this Rick?" Adam asked.

Watch shook his head. "I don't know what happened to him. Bum might, if we can find him. There might also be records in the library that we could check."

Sally made a face. "We have to go to the library? Yuck!"

"What's wrong with the library?" Adam asked reluctantly.

"The librarian's a little strange," Watch said.

"A little?" Sally said. "His name's Mr. Spiney and when he takes your picture for your library card, he actually takes an X-ray. He likes to see your bones when you check out a book, to make sure they're healthy. If you go in the reference room, he locks you inside. Just in case you're thinking of stealing one of his precious magazines or papers. The last time I went in there I was a prisoner for two nights before he let me out. I read the last ten years of *Time* magazine and *Fangoria*."

"I'm glad you put the time to good use," Watch said.

"Mr. Spiney also forces you to drink milk when you're at the library," Sally said. " 'Don't want to let those bones crumble before their time,' he always says. I swear I saw that guy at the cemetery once digging up skeletons. I hear he's got a whole closet full of bones at home."

"Let's not worry about Mr. Spiney," Adam said, not wanting to listen to another weird Sally-Watch conversation. "I want to go to the library." He paused and turned to Cindy. "As long as that's all right with you?"

Cindy nodded sadly, still looking around. "I was hoping so hard I'd find Neil here, waiting for me."

Adam patted her on the back. "We're making progress. That's what's important."

They started to follow Watch down the stairs.

It was then that the searchlight came on.

By mysterious chance, the light was pointed not

out to sea but toward the stairway. Watch was already several steps down the stairs when the light blazed to life, but Cindy was just stepping down into it. Like the rest of them, the sudden light blinded Cindy. Rather than stepping onto the stairway, she stumbled and slid over the side. Adam saw a falling blur off to his left and heard her scream. Not sure what he was doing, he dove to catch her.

The searchlight went off.

Adam saw stars, not much else. But after a second or two he realized he was holding on to one of Cindy's hands, and that she was struggling desperately at the end of it. If she let go, or if he let go of her, she would plunge over a hundred feet to the floor of the lighthouse. Adam screamed for Watch to help.

"Pull her over toward you on the stairway!" Adam called.

"I can't reach her!" Watch shouted back, cleaning his glasses on his shirt. He did have the worst eyes of all of them.

"I'm right here!" Cindy cried. The trapdoor that led into the upper room was fairly wide. Cindy had stumbled off the side opposite the stairway. As Adam's vision cleared, he saw her feet kicking in midair. Sally kneeled by his side and tried to grab Cindy's other hand.

"We won't let you go!" Sally cried.

"You're knocking my hand loose!" Cindy screamed.

"Oh," Sally said, and sat back on her knees. "Sorry."

"Watch," Adam said anxiously, losing his grip on Cindy, "put your glasses back on and reach out and grab her feet. I'm going to lose her."

Watch rubbed his eyes. "I really can't see yet. Cindy, keep talking or screaming or something. I'll hone in on you."

"OK, I can talk," Cindy said breathlessly. "What should I talk about? I've always been afraid of heights. I don't like ghosts much either. But I like ice cream. I like school. I like singing. Some boys."

"Which boys?" Sally asked, climbing back up on her knees.

"Gotcha," Watch said, reaching out and grabbing Cindy's feet.

"Are you sure you've got her?" Adam asked.

"Don't let go of her yet if that's what you're asking," Watch said, pulling Cindy closer.

"That's exactly what he's asking," Cindy said frantically. But just then her feet touched something solid. "Oh. Thank goodness. Is that the stairs below my feet?"

"It better be," Watch said, pulling Cindy farther

over. "It's what I'm standing on. But I still can't see."
Watch pulled her all the way on the stairs. "You're
safe."

Adam let go of Cindy's hand. "Whew," he said.
"That was close." He turned back toward the searchlight and complained to Watch. "I thought you said
the light couldn't come on?"

Watch came back up the steps, Cindy by his side.
Watch studied the wires that led to the searchlight,
but once more shook his head.

"Did you guys touch anything?" Watch asked.

"No," Adam and Sally said.

"I don't see how it turned on," Watch said. "These
wires are shot."

"Could it have another source of power?" Cindy
wondered aloud.

They all looked at one another.

Then they heard a sound.

A faint howling sound.

It seemed to come from far off. From somewhere
out over the ocean. But it wasn't so far away that it
didn't scare them. They hurried down the stairs and
out of the lighthouse. Actually, they ran out of the
place and worked their way back to the jetty on the
rope. They could check it out later, they decided.

Watch couldn't find Bum, so they ended up at the library. To Adam, the place looked more like a ghost house than a place for books. But he was getting used to such things since moving to Spooksville.

Mr. Spiney met them at the door. He had to be the thinnest man Adam had ever seen. Tall and bent, he looked as if his skinny bones were about to burst through his wrinkled skin. He had large hands that looked like claws. He wore an outdated black suit, with vest, and he bowed slightly as he let them inside his library. His voice, when he spoke, made him sound like an old fish.

"Hello children, and welcome," he said. "I do hope your hands are clean and your minds are not dirty. Would you like a glass of milk?"

"No thank you," Sally said quickly. "We're just here to check a few reference materials."

"Sally Wilcox," Mr. Spiney said, peering a little closer. "How nice of you to visit me again." He reached out with one of his clawlike hands. "How are your bones feeling these days?"

Sally took a step back. "Fine, thank you. We don't want any milk and our bones are all perfectly hard and strong. Can we please look at your old newspapers? And can you promise not to lock us inside the reference room?"

Mr. Spiney took a step back and eyed them with a trace of suspicion. "What are you going to do with my newspapers?"

"Just read them," Watch said. "But I wouldn't mind a glass of milk."

Mr. Spiney smiled and nodded. "If you don't drink your milk, you're bound to get osteoporosis." He looked at Cindy and Adam. "Do you know what that is?"

"No," Cindy said.

"And we don't want to know," Adam said.

Mr. Spiney huffed. "Very well. But don't come running to me when your bones begin to crumble. It will be much too late then."

Mr. Spiney led them to a dark room located on the second floor of the library, and then he went to fetch Watch's milk. Sally, of course, believed the milk would be poisonous, but Watch said he was thirsty and didn't care.

Spooksville's official paper was called *The Daily Disaster*. Adam was amazed by how large the obituary section was for such a small town. In each issue, it took up half the paper. Sally was right about one thing: not everyone stayed for long in Spooksville. The cause of death was often listed as simply *disappeared*.

Watch believed they should start searching for information about the lighthouse from thirty years ago.

"Do you know for sure that it closed then?" Cindy asked, helping him get the papers down from the shelves.

"According to Bum it was about then," Watch said.

"What are we looking for anyway?" Sally grumbled. "They don't write about ghosts in the paper. Not even in *The Daily Disaster.*"

"I assume we're looking for the person who turned into the ghost that stole Cindy's brother," Adam said. He glanced at Watch. "Is that right?"

Watch nodded. "I'd be happy to find out who Mommy and Rick were," Watch replied, spreading the papers out on a table in the center of the small dark room.

They searched the papers for more than an hour. During that time Mr. Spiney appeared three times with glasses of milk for everyone. Sally refused to drink any, but Adam and Cindy finally decided to have a little so they wouldn't be rude. Mr. Spiney stood nearby while they sipped. Adam made a face and almost spit out his milk.

"This tastes like it's got sand in it," he complained.

"It's not sand," Mr. Spiney explained. "It's calcium powder. It will make your bones so hard that even when you've been dead and buried twenty years, they'll still be nice and white." He grinned at Cindy and Adam, and for the first time they both noticed what big teeth Mr. Spiney had. "You'll both make beautiful corpses," he said with feeling.

Cindy set her glass down and coughed. "I think I'm getting a milk allergy."

Mr. Spiney finally left them alone, and not long after that Watch uncovered a paper that had an article about the lighthouse.

Double Tragedy at Sea

Last Saturday there was a power failure at the lighthouse. Not long afterward a ship, the *Halifax,* smashed into the reef off Springville and sank. Its captain was listed as Dwayne Pillar. Captain Pillar went down with his ship; his body has yet to be found. What caused the power failure at the lighthouse has not been determined. But the absence of a light was clearly responsible for the wreck of the ship.

By unfortunate chance, the following evening the son of Mrs. Evelyn Maey, the lighthouse keeper, was playing on the jetty beside the lighthouse when a wave washed him out to sea. Five-year-old Rick has yet to be found, and the authorities fear he has drowned. Evelyn Maey was unavailable for comment.

"That's it!" Sally exclaimed.

Everyone looked at her. "What's it?" Watch finally asked.

Sally was excited. "Don't you see? The ghost of Captain Pillar stole Rick because his mother messed up the searchlight and caused the captain's ship to crash. It was his way of getting back at her."

Watch nodded. "That's logical. But what does this ghost have to do with Neil?"

"Yeah," Adam said. "He didn't do anything to the sailor."

Sally spoke with strained patience. "That doesn't matter. Rick was five years old. Neil was five years old. The sailor ghost just likes five-year-old boys. Also, note the time of day Rick was swiped. Near sunset. It was the same time of day Neil disappeared."

"Those are a lot of coincidences," Adam admitted.

"But I thought the old woman's ghost stole Neil," Cindy said.

"What made you think that?" Sally asked.

"Because the ghost that grabbed Neil had hands like an old woman," Cindy said. "She howled like one, too."

"Since when do old women howl?" Sally asked. "Look, we have a clear case of a ghost snatching a boy just like your brother. It's got to be the same ghost. I'd bet my reputation on it."

"That doesn't exactly make you a heavy bettor," Adam muttered.

"Where do you think this sailor ghost is?" Cindy asked, ignoring him.

"He probably lives out on his ship," Sally said.

"Which just happens to be sunk underwater," Adam remarked.

Watch was thoughtful. "But that doesn't mean we can't get to the ship, and that it wouldn't have an air space in it that a person could survive in for a few days. Neil could be there, and alive. They say the *Titanic* had whole rooms that the water didn't get into. And that was underwater a whole lot longer than this ship."

"How do we get to the ship?" Adam asked. "And wouldn't we need scuba equipment."

"I have scuba equipment," Watch said. "I've been diving since I was seven."

"But you can't dive alone in that shark-infested water," Sally said. "It's not safe."

"I have plenty of equipment," Watch said. "I'll take Adam with me."

"But I don't know how to dive," Adam protested.

"I'll teach you," Watch said. "I have a diving certificate. You'll see. It's a lot of fun."

"What if a shark does come?" Cindy asked, although she was clearly excited that they might find her brother.

"He can eat only one of us at a time," Watch said cheerfully.

6

Another hour or so passed before they were able to haul the scuba equipment to the end of the jetty. Adam couldn't believe how heavy the air tanks were. They ended up borrowing a shopping cart from the supermarket to push some of the stuff. But they couldn't take the cart out on the rocky jetty. Adam was exhausted before getting in the water.

"I need to rest," Adam said as he set the tank down next to the rope they had tied to the lighthouse. The equipment looked so complex; he didn't see how he was going to learn to use it in a few minutes. Plus, he couldn't stop thinking about sharks. He didn't want to go through the rest of his life with a nickname like Jaws.

"That might not be a good idea," Watch said. "It's getting late. You want to dive with as much sunlight as possible. The sooner we get in the water the better."

Adam gestured to the equipment. "Will you really be able to teach me how to use all this?"

"You're not chickening out, are you?" Sally asked sweetly.

Adam started to defend himself when Cindy stepped forward and spoke up for him. "Adam's no chicken," she said. "He was the first one to cross over to the lighthouse, in case you've forgotten."

Sally didn't like being challenged by a girl, even one she was supposedly trying to help. She shook a finger in Cindy's face.

"You just remember that it was me who started this whole rescue operation," Sally said. "Besides, Adam and I have been friends a long time. I can call him chicken whenever I want. And he accepts it."

"I wouldn't go that far," Adam said.

"And he's only lived here two weeks," Watch added.

"I just feel like you're jealous of me or something," Cindy said to Sally.

Sally snorted. "Why would I be jealous of you?"

"Cindy should be asking you that question," Adam said.

Sally exploded. "Why do you always take her side?"

"I told you, the sooner we get in the water the better," Watch said.

"I am not always taking her side," Adam said to Sally. "I just think you need to relax a little. That's all. Take things as they come."

Sally smoldered. "We'll see how relaxed you are when a great white shows up."

While getting the scuba equipment at Watch's house, Adam and Watch had picked up swimming trunks. Climbing into the scuba gear, Adam kept asking about each piece of equipment. Watch held up his hand to reassure him.

"I'll adjust all your equipment," Watch said. "All you have to remember is to breathe through your mouth. And don't rush to the surface."

"What happens if I choke and need to get to the surface fast?" Adam asked.

"Your lungs will explode and your face mask will fill with blood," Watch said. "If you choke, cough into your regulator."

"What's that?"

"The thing that goes in your mouth. Also, if you

need to clear your mask, hold the top with one hand and blow out through your nose. The air pressure will expel the water."

Adam was getting nervous. "Does the mask usually fill with water?"

"It can," Watch said.

"Then you couldn't see around you," Sally said darkly. "What's coming for you."

Watch lifted one of the air tanks onto Adam's back. Adam felt as if he were on Jupiter, where gravity was four times greater than on Earth. He could hardly move.

"As soon as you get in the water, you won't feel the weight at all," Watch said. He pointed a hundred yards out to sea. "See where the water changes color right there?"

"Yes," Adam said, panting. Where Watch pointed, the water was a lighter blue.

"That's the beginning of the reef," Watch said. "The ship's probably wrecked somewhere near there. But the reef runs out a quarter mile. We might have to search for a while."

"How long will our air last?" Adam asked, checking the gauge. It read 3000 psi. He hadn't a clue what that meant.

"An hour, if we don't go too deep," Watch said. "When it says zero psi, you're out of air."

"What do we do if we see a shark?" Adam asked.

"Pray," Sally said.

"Go to the bottom," Watch said. "And pray."

Just before Adam climbed in the water, Cindy leaned over and kissed him on the cheek. He had never been kissed by a girl before except his mother, who didn't count. He didn't know what he was supposed to do. He was too scared to kiss her back, especially in front of Sally, who suddenly looked a lot like a shark herself. He just smiled and tried to give her hope.

"Maybe we'll find your brother," Adam said.

Cindy spoke simply, staring at him. "I know you'll find him, Adam."

"Oh brother," Sally muttered. "He'll be lucky if he comes back in one piece." But then Sally acted concerned and touched Adam's arm. "You know, I'm kidding. You be careful, both of you."

"If we really wanted to be careful we wouldn't get in the water," Watch muttered.

They got in the water anyway. Watch let the air out of Adam's BC—his buoyancy control device, whatever that was. Almost immediately Adam began to sink. Yet he didn't panic. He had never been underwater with a mask on before, and he was amazed at how beautiful it was. Different colored fish swam by. The sunlight shining through the surface of the water was like a ray from an alien sun.

They sank steadily and didn't stop until they were down thirty feet. Adam could at least read his depth gauge. Unfortunately, it was much darker than it had been near the surface. Adam could only see ten feet in any direction. Watch bobbled beside him and raised a hand in an OK gesture. Adam flashed back an OK sign.

Watch had been right about one thing. Adam felt completely weightless, as if he were in outer space. It was a great feeling. He was glad he had decided to give it a try.

Watch pointed out toward deeper water, away from the jetty and over to the reef. He wanted Adam to follow. Adam nodded his head. It was interesting communicating without talking.

They moved forward. Adam quickly discovered that he swam faster if he didn't use his arms, just his fins. He felt very comfortable under the water, and his fear of sharks almost went away. He watched as his silver bubbles rose slowly to the surface. He wondered if Cindy and Sally could see their bubbles.

Two minutes later they were at the reef. They were

now forty-five feet down, and it was as dark as half an hour after sunset. The reef was not made of coral, but of jagged rock. Watch had explained that coral only grew in warm water. As they drifted over it, searching for signs of a wrecked ship, Adam imagined he was floating over the surface of a distant moon. Even though it was dark, up close the beautiful colors remained. He wished he had a camera to take pictures to show his family. He knew they wouldn't believe his story without proof. He wouldn't have believed it himself.

Watch handed Adam a flashlight. Adam didn't know why he hadn't given it to him on the surface, but figured Watch must have been afraid he would lose it before he grew comfortable underwater. The flashlights were small, not very powerful, but the beams lit up the rocks somewhat. Watch flashed his light in and out of the crevasses for any sign of the wreck.

They had been searching the reef for maybe thirty minutes when Adam suddenly felt something slide down his front. Looking down, he realized Watch had not tightened his weight belt enough. It was about to slip off. The weights, Adam knew, helped hold him down. He had not forgotten his lungs would explode if he rushed to the surface. A wave of terror swept over him. Instead of grabbing the slipping belt, he grabbed Watch's arm and pointed frantically at what was happening.

Watch looked over.

At that moment Adam's weight belt fell off completely.

The belt sank like a rock, disappearing into a deep crevasse.

Adam felt himself begin to float upward. Quickly.

Oh no, Adam thought. His lungs would explode.

Soon he would see his blood. *Yuck.*

He would die. The fish would have him for food.

But Watch grabbed him and pulled him down hard, shaking his head. Adam didn't need the lecture. He knew he was supposed to go up slowly. But without the weights, it seemed impossible to stay down. But drag him down Watch did, until they were floating beside the top of the reef. Watch reached over, grabbed a rock, and stuffed it in one of the pockets on Adam's BC. Immediately Adam sank down, and Watch was able to let him go. Watch pointed to the place where the weight belt had disappeared and then pointed to himself. He was going to search for the belt. Adam was to wait for him. Adam nodded vigorously.

Watch disappeared.

Adam sat on the edge of the reef and wondered if it was logical to be searching for a ghost in shark-infested waters. With Watch gone, it was hard to stop thinking about sharks. He had heard that great whites could weigh more than three thousand pounds. The shark could have Adam for a snack and still be hungry. He wished Watch would hurry and get back with his weight belt.

But Watch didn't come back.

Ten minutes went by. Fifteen.

Still no Watch.

Adam checked his air gauge: 500 psi. He assumed that meant he was almost out of air. He had to start back soon, but how could he without Watch? Sally would yell at him and call him a chicken again. Besides, he liked Watch and didn't think his friend would leave him alone on purpose.

Adam's air gauge sank to 400 psi, then 300 psi.

He would need what little air he had left to make it back to the surface.

Maybe a shark got Watch.

Adam groaned behind his face mask, unsure of what to do.

It was then that he saw the wreck.

At first he wasn't sure what it was. Just a glimmer of white in the eerie blue-black. It was off to his left, almost behind him, which was why he hadn't seen it earlier. But it didn't look that far away; it couldn't be if he was able to see it at all. He wondered if Watch had seen it on the way back from retrieving the weight belt. Maybe Watch was already inside the wreck, Adam thought. That would explain why he hadn't returned.

Adam made a decision. He would check out the boat for one minute, no more. Then he had to head back up, with or without Watch.

Adam swam slowly toward the wreck.

It grew in size. The boat had been a motor yacht maybe sixty feet long. Adam could see the gash in the front where the hull had hit the rocks. He had to assume that farther out the rocks were closer to the surface. He could even read the faint lettering on the side. Thirty years had not washed it away. He was definitely looking at the *Halifax.*

Adam checked his air: 200 psi.

He had to return to the surface. Now.

But just as he turned to swim up, he thought he saw several small bubbles float out of the hole in the hull. The opening was three feet across. He wondered if Watch had swum inside and become stuck. If that was true, Watch's air would be running out.

Adam made another hard decision.

He would swim into the hole.

Just a quick look around and then back out.

But Adam had to dive down slightly to reach the hole. He was now fifty-five feet underwater, and he vaguely remembered Watch saying he had to stop for three minutes at fifteen feet before going to the surface. Well, Adam thought, that was one stop he wouldn't have time to make. Maybe his lungs would explode after all. Yet he wasn't as scared as he had been earlier. He had to save his friend. He was doing what he had to do.

Adam swam into the crack in the hull.

His flashlight was out in front of him. He swam into the bow of the boat, into a storage room of some kind. He disturbed a mop and pail, and they floated up. The walls closed around him and it seemed that his light dimmed. He hoped Watch had checked the batteries before they went under. He hoped he found Watch soon. The storage room was partially crushed, and the way was narrow. Adam imagined how easy it would be to get stuck inside, without being able to turn around.

Something jumped out at him.

It had sharp teeth. Big eyes. An ugly face.

Adam screamed inside his mask.

He dropped his flashlight.

Everything went dark. Perfectly black.

Oh-no. Oh-no. Oh-no.

At that moment Adam knew he was doomed. The horrible creature coming toward him was about to take a big bite out of his face, and then it would crawl through the hole and eat his brains. For several terrifying seconds Adam floated frozen, waiting to be devoured by the monster from the deep.

Yet the seconds ticked by and nothing bit him. Also, when he finally opened his eyes, he realized that his flashlight had not gone out. It was floating just below his feet. Only the beam was pointing into a closet and was no longer lighting up the storage area. It had gone black because he had almost blacked out.

Adam reached down and grabbed his light.

He saw the creature again.

And screamed again.

Then he stopped, embarrassed.

The creature looked scary, but it wasn't that big. He realized he was looking at a one-foot-long electric eel, which was similar to an underwater snake. The little eel actually seemed more terrified of him. Adam flicked his hand once, and the thing darted away. Now Adam decided it was time for him to get away. If Watch had entered the wreck, he wasn't there now.

Adam turned and swam back the way he'd come.

He thought he was going back the way he'd come.

But he didn't emerge back into the ocean.

Instead, he found himself in a stateroom.

He floated up into it and shone his light around.

He must have gotten turned around.

Probably when he closed his eyes and screamed into his mask.

Adam noticed something funny about the large stateroom. It was filled with air. It was a good thing. Adam checked his own air supply. Again he almost fainted. His panic attack with the electric eel had drained his tank.

He had 0 psi.

Adam gagged on the regulator in his mouth.

It was not giving him any more air.

He pulled it out of his mouth and drew in a deep breath. The air in the stateroom was old and smelled like fish. But at least it fed his lungs; he wasn't about to complain. Adam couldn't believe how he had gotten himself into such a mess. He was fifty-five feet underwater and his tank was completely empty. Worse, no one knew where he was.

Adam searched around some more with his flashlight.

It was then that he saw something worse than an electric eel.

A million times worse.

It was a slimy skull. A whole skeleton.

It floated toward him.

Adam screamed. No one heard him.

And the skeleton kept coming.

7

"**I** lost him," Watch said as he climbed back onto the jetty.

"What?" Sally screamed. "How could you lose him?"

Watch sat on a boulder and pulled his face mask off. "He dropped his weight belt and I went down to retrieve it. But it was stuck between two rocks. I had a hard time getting it loose. When I finally returned to where I'd left Adam, he wasn't there." Watch glanced around. "I don't suppose either of you has seen him?"

"Of course we haven't seen him!" Sally yelled. "You were supposed to take care of him!"

"I'm sorry," Watch said.

"You're sorry!" Sally cried. "You just murdered my future senior prom date!"

"It's a long time till senior year," Watch said. "You might meet someone else you like."

Cindy had tears in her eyes. "Is Adam really dead?" she asked.

Watch hung his head sadly. "I'm completely out of air. He has to be, too. Unless he grew gills in the last few minutes, I don't see how he can be alive." Watch looked out to sea and sighed. "He was so young."

Cindy put her hand to her head. "Oh no. This is all my fault. Poor Adam."

"Stop sobbing," Sally snapped at Cindy. "It ain't over till it's over." Sally paused to think. "Why would Adam have left the spot where you left him? We have to ask ourselves this question."

Watch shrugged. "Maybe a shark got him."

Cindy wept louder.

"Would you please quit being so depressing!" Sally yelled.

"But you're the one who's been talking about sharks all day," Watch said.

"That was before Adam was missing." Sally froze suddenly and then snapped her fingers. "I got it! Adam left the spot where you last saw him because he saw the wreck. It's the only explanation."

"I didn't see the wreck," Watch said, rubbing the water off his thick glasses, which he had worn under his custom-made mask.

"Yeah, but you're half blind," Sally said, pacing. "This is logical. And if Adam did go inside the wreck, there's a good chance he found an air pocket. He could still be alive. We have to get more air. We have to go back down for him."

"We?" Watch asked.

"Yes," Sally said proudly. "I will risk my life to save Adam because my love for him is more powerful than my fear of death." She stopped and glared at crying Cindy. "I bet you can't say the same thing."

Cindy wiped at her face. "I don't mind going after him."

Watch nodded. "You two go while I rest."

Sally threw another tantrum. "You have to go because you're the only one who knows where you left him! You have to go back to that spot and search for the wreck. It has to be in that area." Sally paused. "Actually, you'll have to go alone. We don't have any more scuba equipment."

"So much for your brave promise to save Adam," Cindy said.

Sally sneered. "It's the thought that counts. But you can rest for a few minutes, Watch, while Cindy and I get you another air tank. Come on, Cindy, and quit sassing me. Adam's life is all that matters now."

Watch nodded. "I'll stay here to see if any huge trails of blood float to the surface."

Sally shook her head as she walked away. "Somehow I get the feeling you don't know what a positive attitude means," she said.

Adam had stopped screaming. The reason the skeleton had been rushing toward him was because—in his panic—he had been splashing in the water and created a mild current inside the stateroom. This had set the skeleton free to float toward him. The skeleton was not alive, after all, but as dead as any other creature that had gone down with the ship. Too bad Mr. Spiney wasn't around to inspect it, Adam thought. The librarian probably would have loved the old sailor's strong white bones.

Adam didn't know if anyone was coming to his

rescue. He hoped someone was because he didn't like to think what his bones would look like after he'd been rotting in the ship for a few years. He didn't know what he could do to help his friends locate him. He wished Watch had given him a flare gun along with the flashlight. One thing was sure, he knew he couldn't swim to the surface without another tank of air. He'd just have to be patient.

While waiting, Adam studied the contents of the stateroom, trying to get an idea of what Captain Pillar had been like. Just looking at his skeleton didn't tell Adam much. There were the usual things one would expect to be floating about: books, chairs, boxes of food, and cans of soup. But the most dominant item in the yacht was booze. It seemed that Captain Pillar had gone to sea with gallons of alcohol. Indeed, when Adam examined the skeleton closer he saw that Captain Pillar had plunged to his watery grave tightly clutching a bottle of whiskey. Even in death, he couldn't give up the stuff.

It made Adam wonder if the broken lighthouse had had anything to do with the wreck of the ship. Adam was pretty sure Captain Pillar had been so drunk that dark night thirty years ago that he hadn't known where he was going, searchlight or no searchlight. If

Captain Pillar's ghost had swiped Neil, it had no right to do it.

But Adam was almost positive there was no Neil down here. And he had a feeling that there never had been. Sally had jumped to her conclusion too fast. Adam doubted that Captain Pillar had anything to do with the disappearance of the boy. At least not directly.

Adam just hoped he lived to tell his friends about his important observations.

Time went by, and Adam began to get cold. He had on a wet suit, of course, but it didn't keep him nearly so warm now that he'd stopped swimming. But he couldn't move around too much because he'd use up the air quicker.

He had another problem. The battery in his flashlight was dying. Every minute or so, the light would briefly flicker out. Each time it came back on, it was slightly dimmer. The underwater boat was spooky enough with light. In the dark, Adam didn't know if he'd be able to stand it. The cold would seep into his heart and lungs, and he wouldn't even be able to shout for help. He reconsidered. Maybe he should try to make one last dash for the surface. If his lungs exploded, at least it would be over for him soon.

But Adam stayed where he was.

He didn't want his lungs to explode.

He was sure it would hurt real bad.

More time passed. His light flickered.

But this time it didn't come back on.

"Oh no," Adam whispered as he shook the flashlight. He played with the switch, turning it on and off. But it remained off.

He was alone, in the dark. Underwater with a dead sailor.

"This is worse than the Secret Path," Adam whispered as he began to shiver. He'd never been in such a cold black place. He tried to think back to how it had all got started. Really, he'd just wanted his big excitement that day to be doughnuts and milk.

"Yeah, but you wanted to be the big hero, too," he told himself. That was the trouble with most movies and books, he decided. They didn't tell the stories of all the heroes who didn't live to tell their tales. He doubted there would even be an article in *The Daily Disaster* to describe his brave attempt to save Neil.

"It's a stupid name for a paper anyway," Adam said between trembling teeth.

More time went by. Adam began to lose the feeling in his hands, his feet. His constant shivering was slowly being replaced by a strange drowsy warm feeling. He knew that was a bad sign. He was getting hypothermia—he had read about it in one of his mother's magazines. He would pass out soon, and drown, and the fish would eat him. It was a cruel world. It was a weird town.

Then he saw a strange yellow light. He wondered if that meant he was dead, that an angel was coming to take him to heaven. He thought he deserved to go there since he had died so bravely. The light was coming up beneath him and it was getting so very bright. He wondered if his guardian angel would be fat and naked like the ones in the old paintings. He sort of hoped he had a nicer-looking angel, not that he was picky.

But it wasn't an angel.

A human head popped up out of the water.

"Watch," Adam said softly. "What are you doing here?"

Watch took out his regulator and pulled off his face mask. "I've come to rescue you."

"You took long enough," Adam said, although he was happy to see his friend.

"Sorry. I sent the girls for another air tank but they brought back a huge bottle of laughing gas instead. The dive shop in Spooksville also supplies the local dentists. They often get their inventory mixed up. I had to go back to the shop myself." Watch searched around with his flashlight and nodded in the direction of Captain Pillar's skeleton, which was still holding on to its whiskey bottle. "Is that the guy whose ghost stole Neil?" Watch asked.

"I don't think so," Adam replied. "I really think the ghost is up in the lighthouse. I think there's only one ghost. Remember that howling we heard? And there was no way that searchlight could have come on by itself."

Adam went on to explain his theory that the boat had crashed because the captain had been drunk, not because the searchlight was off. Watch thought that made sense. But he wanted to bring the skeleton with them anyway.

"Why?" Adam asked.

"Because you never know," Watch said. "The ghost in the lighthouse might want to talk to it."

Adam snickered. "Skeletons can't talk."

"Yeah, and ghosts aren't supposed to exist. Don't forget where you're living. I wouldn't be surprised if the skeleton and the ghost got in a big argument. It won't be the first time that's happened around here."

Adam yawned. "We can take it with us if you want. If nothing else, we can give it to Mr. Spiney." He pointed to Watch's air tank. "Did you bring me an extra tank?"

"No. But you don't need it. We can buddy breathe."

"Is that dangerous?" Adam asked.

"Not if just two people are doing it together." Watch glanced again at the skeleton. "I don't think he needs any air."

9

Sally and Cindy were overjoyed to see Adam alive. Adam was surprised at how glad they were. They both had tears in their eyes as he climbed onto the rocks, although Sally quickly brushed hers away. Adam felt pleased to know he would have been missed if he'd died. This hero business did have its rewards. Not that he wanted another kiss or anything gross like that.

"If it wasn't for me, you would still be down there with the fish," Sally said. "I was the one who figured

out where you were. I never lost hope, even as Cindy
and Watch were planning your funeral."

"That's not true," Cindy said. "In my heart I knew
Adam would pull through."

"Yeah, that's why you picked out a tank of laughing
gas instead of air," Sally said.

Cindy was insulted. "You chose a tank with a skull
and crossbones on it."

"Speaking of bones," Watch said, with Captain
Pillar in tow. "This is what Adam found in the ship.
Don't worry, Cindy, it's not your brother."

"I can see that," Cindy said, looking a little sick.
The skeleton was draped with seaweed, and there was
a tiny crab crawling out of one of its eye sockets.
"There was no sign of my brother?" Cindy asked
quietly.

"No," Adam said. "But I think we've been chasing
after the wrong ghost. We have to search the lighthouse again."

"But we already searched it," Sally protested. "Neil
wasn't inside. I would—"

"Bet my reputation on it," Watch finished for her.

"We hardly searched the place before leaving,"
Adam said. "What if the top floor had an attic above
it?"

Watch nodded as he stared up at the top of the lighthouse. "There could be a tiny room above the searchlight. At least it looks that way from here." Watch shivered. "But it's getting late and I'm hungry. Maybe we should try to save Neil tomorrow, after a warm meal and a good night's sleep."

Cindy was agitated. "But you really think my brother might be stuck in there with an evil ghost?" she asked Adam. "If it's true, I can't leave him there another night."

"For all we know the ghost might be enjoyable company," Watch said. "Remember Casper. He wasn't a bad fellow."

"He was a whiner," Sally disagreed. "He was always complaining about being dead. He should have had to live in Spooksville for a few weeks, see what we go through. Then he would have stopped his moaning."

Adam shook his head. "We have to go back inside the lighthouse and we have to go now. Before it gets completely dark."

"Should we bring the skeleton?" Watch asked.

"It might look nice hung up beside the spider webs," Sally said.

"I don't care if you bring it," Adam said. "Just get this scuba equipment off my back."

The girls crossed over to the lighthouse on the rope. Watch and Adam were still in their trunks and they swam. This time they had a flashlight. It was good because the sun had set while Adam was trapped underwater. Just as they stepped inside the lighthouse, Sally reminded them that all the bad things that had occurred had happened at this exact time of day.

"You don't have to wait till midnight to see a ghost in this town," Sally said.

Adam was relieved to get inside. The interior of the lighthouse was much warmer than the jetty, and he was able to stop shivering. But it was more than comfort that encouraged him. Adam felt as if they were finally closing in on Neil. What had happened in the lighthouse earlier had scared them. That was why they hadn't come back right away. But after his terror below the sea, Adam felt ready to face anything.

They started up the long spiral staircase. Like the last time, it was hard climbing. Soon they were hot and sweating. But no one asked to stop and rest. Watch continued to drag the skeleton with him. Remarkably, the dead captain still managed to have a hold of his whiskey bottle.

After about ten minutes they reached the trapdoor

that led into the upper level. Watch raised his hand for them to stop.

"Now remember," Watch said, "if the searchlight suddenly comes on, close your eyes. We don't want you to stumble around. You might fall down this opening."

"I won't do that again," Cindy said, anxious to keep going.

They entered the upper level. Watch set the skeleton down and studied the wires on the searchlight again. The rest of them examined the wooden ceiling, something they hadn't thought to do before. Adam focused the flashlight on several grooved lines in the wood.

"Those look like they could be the outline of a door of some kind," Adam said, pointing.

"But how are we going to get up there?" Sally asked. "And how are we going to open the door? There's no knob, no lock."

"Let me go up first and check it out," Adam said. He tapped Watch on the shoulder. "Help me shove that desk over, and then I'll put that chair on top of it."

Watch studied the ceiling. "You still won't be able to reach it."

"I will if I stand on your shoulders," Adam said.

Watch was impressed. "If you fall, you'll break your neck." He added, "You might pull me down with you."

"It's a risk we'll have to take," Adam said firmly.

"There he goes trying to impress Cindy again," Sally muttered.

"I'll follow you up into the attic, Adam," Cindy said, interrupting Sally with a nasty look.

Together they moved the desk. Watch and Adam climbed onto the desk, and Sally and Cindy handed them the chair. Watch carefully positioned the chair and got up on it, taking a moment to balance himself.

"How much do you weigh?" Watch asked Adam.

Adam shrugged. "I don't know. Less than you."

"If you fall, don't grab my hair," Watch said. "And tuck the flashlight in your belt. But keep it on."

Adam did as he was told. Then he looked back up at Watch. "How am I supposed to get up on your shoulders?" he asked.

"It's your plan," Sally muttered.

"Climb up on the chair beside me," Watch said. Again, Adam did what he was told. "Good. Now give me your foot. I'll boost you up. Remember what I said about my hair."

"If I lose my balance, can I at least grab your ears?" Adam asked.

"I suppose," Watch said. "Just don't pull too hard. I don't want to have to go to the hospital to have them sewn back on."

"Spooksville's main hospital is located only a block from the cemetery," Sally said. "And there's a good reason. There's a surgeon who works there who has this thing about people's spare parts. Every time he operates, he tries to get out all the spare parts. I know this kid at school, Craig, who went into the hospital to have his tonsils out. And this surgeon removed one of Craig's lungs while he was at it. Now we all call Craig *Breathless.*" Sally added, "But at least he doesn't have to take PE anymore."

"What's this surgeon's name?" Adam asked, thinking if he ever got sick he'd be sure his parents didn't request him.

"Dr. Jonathan Smith," Sally said. "But the hospital staff just calls him *Dr. Ripper.*"

"Could we please have a little less history," Cindy said. "And a little more action."

Sally was insulted. "You haven't lived here long. At times like this, a little knowledge of Spooksville might save your life. Why I remember one time this troll was—"

"I'm going up," Adam interrupted. "Ready, Watch?"

Watch clasped his hands together for Adam to step on. "Ready. The second you step on my shoulders, brace your arm on the ceiling. That should keep you from falling."

Adam hesitated. "You don't have to sneeze or anything?"

"No."

"Good." Adam set his foot in Watch's cupped hands, and Watch boosted him up. With his other foot Adam immediately stepped up and onto Watch's shoulder. For an instant he wobbled dangerously, and he was sure he was going to fall. The floor suddenly seemed so far away. It would be weird to almost drown and then fall to your death in the same day, Adam thought.

"Grab the ceiling!" Watch shouted.

Adam threw his right hand up and touched the ceiling. Actually, there was nothing to grab because the wood was relatively smooth. But, as Watch had said, he was able to brace himself by pressing against the ceiling. In a moment he had regained his balance.

Adam panted. "That was close."

"You weigh a lot more than most twelve-year-olds," Watch grumbled.

"I'm not that big," Adam said.

"You have high density," Watch replied. "I can't hold you long. Study the grooves. Look for a way in."

Adam didn't have to study anything. The moment he touched the space between the grooves, a three-foot-wide panel pushed up into the ceiling. Grabbing the edge with one hand, Adam carefully reached for his flashlight with the other and focused it into the opening.

"Do you see anything?" Cindy asked, anxiously.

"Darkness," Adam said honestly. "I'll have to climb up into the space."

"Be careful," Cindy whispered.

"The time for care has passed," Sally said ominously.

Adam tucked the flashlight back into his belt to keep both hands free. Telling Watch to be extra still, he moved his hands so that he was grabbing the corner of the opening. Counting to three, he yanked up hard with his arms, pulling his body off Watch's shoulders. But he wasn't able to throw his legs into the opening. Suddenly he was dangling in midair, without support. Watch had climbed down from the chair onto the desktop.

"Why did you leave me?" Adam gasped, barely holding on.

"I was afraid you'd kick me in the head," Watch said.

"Don't let go," Cindy called anxiously.

"That's good advice," Sally said sarcastically.

Adam realized that he couldn't hang there all night. His arms were tiring quickly. Taking a deep breath, he tried pulling himself up again. This time he managed to catch the other corner of the opening with one foot. That was all the leverage he needed. A moment later he was sitting on the floor of the dark attic. There were no windows, and no light from the moon or stars got through. The others gathered below him.

"Is my brother there?" Cindy called up.

"Just let me have a look around," Adam said, moving the beam of the flashlight across the room. He had hardly begun to search when a glimpse of a hideous skeleton sitting in a rocking chair jumped out at him. Adam was so startled that he let out a cry and dropped the flashlight.

"Ahhh!" he shouted.

In fact, he dropped the flashlight through the opening in the ceiling.

Luckily, Watch caught it.

"Do you see something interesting?" Sally asked casually.

Adam hugged the edges of the opening and frantically listened for the approach of the skeleton. From his experience on the Secret Path, he knew there were dead people—the good ones—who stayed dead, and dead people—the bad ones—who liked to play with the living. But it was hard to hear anything because his heart was pounding so loud and he was choking on the last breath he had taken.

"What's happening?" Cindy shouted, worried.

"There's a dead person up here," Adam croaked.

"Is that all?" Sally said.

"Is this dead person trying to kill you?" Watch asked matter-of-factly.

"I don't know." Adam gasped. He would have leaped back down to the desk if he hadn't been sure he would break his neck. He continued to hug the edges of the opening, waiting for a bony hand to settle on his shoulder and rip open his flesh. But after a minute or so into his latest nervous breakdown, nothing happened. Adam finally began to breathe easier. The skeleton wasn't moving.

"Are you under attack?" Sally asked.

"I'm fine," Adam said finally.

"He's fine," Sally said to the others. "He's scared out of his pants, but he's fine."

"Can you throw the flashlight up to me?" Adam asked Watch.

"Sure," Watch said. Carefully, he tossed the flashlight straight up and through the opening. Adam was lucky to catch it on the first try. After a moment's hesitation, Adam focused the light back on the skeleton. She was not a pretty sight, even by a skeleton's standards.

Her hair was long and stringy. It looked like straw that had been dipped in white paint, then left out in the wind to dry. She wore the shreds of a violet dress—that the bugs had been nibbling at for the last thirty years. The wooden chair she sat in looked as if it was about to collapse.

But the most scary thing was her face, or what was left of it. Her jaw hung open. Her few remaining teeth were cracked and gray and yellow. The empty sockets of her eyes glared at him. The darkness inside them seemed particularly deep and cold. Adam had to force himself not to stare. He almost felt as if he were being hypnotized.

Adam realized he was looking at Evelyn Maey.

Last caretaker of Spooksville's lighthouse. Mother of lost Rick.

"Is my brother there?" Cindy asked again.

"I don't see him," Adam replied. "But—"

"But what?" Sally asked when Adam didn't finish his sentence.

Adam cocked his head to the side. "I think I hear something."

"What?" they all asked at the same time.

"I'm not sure," Adam said. The sound was faint, but not far. It was not a howling noise, but something that was equally disturbing. If it belonged to a hungry monster.

Adam thought he heard footsteps. But only for a moment.

He played the light over the attic space.

Nothing beside Mrs. Maey. The sound was gone.

"What's happening?" Sally demanded.

"Nothing," Adam muttered, puzzled.

"Nothing's happening," Sally told the others. "And yet he's driving us crazy with suspense."

"I want to come up there," Cindy said.

"How much do you weigh?" Watch asked, rubbing his shoulders.

"I don't know if you want to bother, Cindy," Adam said. "There's a pretty ugly skeleton up here."

"Like we have a good-looking one down here," Sally said.

"I have to go up there," Cindy insisted.

Watch sighed. "Just don't pull on any of my parts if you lose your balance."

Watch and Cindy climbed up on the chair, and then Watch boosted her up to the ceiling. Because Adam was able to reach down and help her, Cindy didn't have nearly as much trouble getting into the attic as he had. A moment later she was sitting on the dusty floor beside him. Adam pointed the flashlight at Mrs. Maey. Cindy gasped.

"She's ugly," she whispered.

"Dying can do that to you," Adam remarked as he stood up.

Just then several terrifying things happened at once.

The wooden door that led into the attic fell shut.

Cindy tried to pull it back open.

But it was locked tight.

Down below, beside Sally and Watch, the huge searchlight began to move until it was pointed straight up, toward the ceiling.

"What's happening?" Sally screamed.

The searchlight came on.

The light was blinding. Sally and Watch staggered back, covering their eyes. The light was so powerful it pierced through the fine space between the attic boards. As a result, Adam and Cindy—now cut off from their friends—were also blinded. It was as if a sun had just been born under their feet. He grabbed Cindy and pulled her close.

"The trapdoor won't open!" she cried.

"Did you knock it shut?" Adam yelled back.

Because he had to yell to be heard.

Because suddenly there was a loud howling.

As if the ocean wind were breaking in.

Or a ghost was coming to life.

"No!" Cindy cried. "It shut by itself."

"Watch!" Adam called, dropping once more to his knees, trying to pull up the trapdoor. It was more than stuck. It didn't budge; it could have been nailed shut. "Sally!"

They didn't answer. Or if they did their voices were drowned out by the howling. Yet, as he stood and shielded his eyes to look around, Adam knew it was no wind that was making that sound. The attic dust continued to remain undisturbed. No breeze could come in from the outside. The sound was supernatural in origin. They had found their ghost, and it was probably a mistake that Cindy had said how ugly the skeleton was.

Because the ghost was coming back to life.

Where the blinding rays of the searchlight swept the skeleton, Adam saw a strange form begin to take shape. It appeared to be made of both light and dust, as if it drew to it whatever was handy to make its form. As the noise reached a deafening pitch and the walls of the attic began to shake, both Adam and Cindy saw the ghost of an old lady materialize where the skeleton sat.

The skeleton did not vanish. They could still see it, but through the haze of the old lady ghost. And all of a sudden the skeleton didn't look so scary. Because the ghost that stirred in its place was a thousand times worse. It glared at them with strange violet eyes that flashed cold fire. It raised both its arms, and its wrinkled hands were like claws. The razor-sharp nails that bent from the twisted fingertips made Cindy squeal. She had obviously seen those hands before.

"That's the ghost that stole my brother!" she yelled.

"I'm not surprised." Adam gulped. He put an arm around Cindy and carefully pulled her back, away from the ghost, which had climbed to its feet. For a moment the thing searched the attic. But then its angry eyes settled back on them, and it took a step in their direction. Cindy shook in Adam's arms, and he was not feeling exactly strong himself.

"What do you think it wants," Cindy said, gasping.

"One of us," Adam whispered. "Maybe both."

Just then they heard the cries of a young boy.

The sound came from even farther above them.

The attic had an attic.

"Neil!" Cindy cried. "That's my brother." She let go of Adam and strode toward the ghost, anger in her step. "You old ugly ghost!" she swore at the thing. "You give me back my brother!"

"You might not want to insult it," Adam suggested. "Try saying please."

But Cindy was too furious. Overhead, her brother continued to shout, pounding on the ceiling. It was only then that Adam noticed a ladder pinned to the ceiling. Obviously, it could be used to reach the second attic. If he could get to it. Between him and the ladder stood the ghost, and the thing didn't look in the best of moods. Cindy raised a finger and shook it in the ghost's face.

"You had no right to take him," Cindy said. "He never did anything to you." Cindy paused and shouted at the ceiling. "We're coming, Neil!"

"Try getting around to its other side," Adam whispered loudly.

Cindy glanced over her shoulder. "Why?"

"Just do it," Adam said. "I'll explain later. Keep it distracted."

Cindy nodded and turned back to the ghost, which

still looked angry, but unsure of what to do with them. Cindy moved to Adam's right. The ghost followed her. Adam began to move to the left.

"Just let Neil go and I won't file criminal charges," Cindy told the ghost. "We can forget the whole thing, pretend it never happened."

The ghost fixed its attention on Cindy. It even moved as she moved. Adam was able to use the opportunity to jump up and grab one end of the ladder. It folded down smoothly, barely creaking. Adam felt a wave of triumph. If he could get up into the second attic and grab Neil, they could be out of here and home in time for dinner. He pushed one end of the ladder to the floor and started up the steps. There was another trapdoor above with a metal catch. He'd have no trouble opening it.

Adam almost made it. Another couple of steps and he'd have reached Neil. But the ghost was not blind.

Adam felt a strong hard hand grip his ankle.

He glanced down, not really wanting to see what had a hold of him.

The ghost glared up at him. Fire burned in its violet eyes as it growled. The other hand wrapped around his other ankle. Then he was falling. The ghost had pulled his feet out from under him.

Adam hit the floor hard. Pain flared through his

right side, and he had trouble drawing in a breath. Before he could recover, the ghost was on him. It was awfully strong for an old woman, especially one that had been dead thirty years.

It grabbed him by the arms and lifted him right off the floor. For a moment Adam stared directly into its face. He could still see through it, but it seemed with each passing second the ghost was becoming more solid. It actually had bad breath. It gloated over him and then threw its head back, opening its mouth wide. The howling again shook the attic.

"Maybe we could discuss this," Adam said. "Work out some kind of trade."

The ghost was not in the mood to talk. It carried Adam to the wall, and with one stiff kick it broke a hole in the wall. Adam felt the cold air pour in. The ghost gave another kick and a large section of the wall collapsed. The ghost pushed Adam through the opening. Far below him—one hundred feet at least—he saw the waves crashing against jagged boulders. The wind tossed his hair. The ghost was slowly loosening its hold on him. This was it, he thought, he was going to die. No way could he survive such a fall.

"Adam!" Cindy cried.

The ghost dropped him.

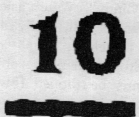

10

eanwhile Sally and Watch were very busy themselves. When the searchlight first came on, they both stumbled around half blind, doing exactly what Watch himself had warned them not to do. This time Sally almost stepped into the trapdoor opening and fell. But Watch bumped into her at that moment. They decided to close the trapdoor.

"What's happening?" Sally repeated. "What's that howling sound?"

"I think the ghost has woken up," Watch said, holding a hand up like a visor to block out the light.

They heard shouts above, but couldn't understand what was being said. "We have to rescue Adam!" Sally cried.

"What about Cindy?" Watch asked.

"We can save her as well," Sally said. "Quick, go up on the desk and the chair."

"No." Watch stopped her. "It's obvious the ghost is up there. They must be trapped. If we go up, we'll just get trapped."

"You're a coward," Sally said. "We can't just leave them."

"I'm not saying we should leave them," Watch said. "But I think this is a powerful ghost. It was able to grab Neil all the way at the far end of the jetty. We have to strike at the heart of its power."

"What's that?" Sally asked.

Watch pointed to the blindingly bright light. "This. Every time the ghost appears, the searchlight comes on."

"You're right!" Sally exclaimed. "Let's bust the bulbs."

It sounded simple enough. The problem was that when Watch lifted the chair to smash the searchlight, he couldn't get near it. The chair struck the beam of light as if it were striking a forcefield. The wood shattered in his hands and splinters went flying everywhere. Watch staggered back and would have fallen if Sally hadn't grabbed him.

"I think the searchlight is haunted as well," Sally said.

Watch straightened up and nodded. "But I still think we can disable it. Remember Adam said there were cans of kerosene in the storage room downstairs? I didn't have a chance to look, but I think this light is powered by a generator inside the lighthouse. Maybe in that very storage room. The generator probably runs on kerosene. The wiring from it must come straight up under the floor. I know for a fact the old city wiring is not giving this thing any juice. The wires are too worn out."

"What are you going to do?" Sally asked.

"I want to run downstairs and wreck the generator. I hope that'll turn off the searchlight, and shut up the ghost."

"That's great," Sally said. "But what am I supposed to do?"

Watch glanced up at the ceiling. There was so much noise up there; it didn't sound like Adam and Cindy were having an easy time with the ghost.

"Maybe there's something you can do to slow the ghost down until I get to the generator," he said.

"Tell me!" Sally demanded.

"I've been thinking about that article we read in the library. It listed the caretaker's name as Evelyn Maey. And we know her son's name was Rick."

"So?"

"You know the staff at *The Daily Disaster*. They always mess up the facts a little. What if they accidentally left off the letter *k*. What if their last name was really Makey."

Sally blinked. "Like in Cindy Makey?"

"Yes. When we were getting the scuba equipment, Cindy told me her father's name was Frederick, but her mother just called him Fred. But what if her father's *mother* had called him Rick?"

Wonder dawned on Sally's face. "Are you saying that Cindy's father might have been the boy who washed out to sea thirty years ago?"

"Yes. Notice where Cindy lives now. In her father's house, which is right next to the lighthouse."

"That's right! Cindy must be the granddaughter of the ghost! Watch, you're a genius!"

"I've known that since I was four years old."

"Wait a second," Sally said. "The paper said the boy, Rick, was never found."

"And Cindy said her father was raised an orphan. The guy probably washed out to sea and didn't wash up again until he was halfway to San Francisco. It's no surprise he never made it back home."

"And Mrs. Makey died without knowing her son was alive," Sally said, nodding to herself. "That's what's made her such a bitter old ghost."

"That and living here, I think," Watch said.

Sally had one last doubt. "But Frederick must have come back to Spooksville as an adult to claim his mother's house. He must have known where it was."

"Maybe the memory of Spooksville only came back to him as he got older," Watch said.

Sally nodded. "Maybe his foster parents were nicer than that old bag upstairs. He probably didn't want to come home."

"Spooksville's a hard town to come home to," Watch agreed.

They heard a big thump above them.

It sounded like a body had hit the floor.

"You get to the generator," Sally said to Watch. "I'll deal with the ghost."

Watch hurried down the stairs. Sally searched for another entrance to the attic. Outside, beyond the windows through which the searchlight normally shone, was a wooden balcony. Sally had noticed it earlier, from the outside, but had forgotten about it in all the excitement. She wondered if she could climb up onto the rails of the balcony and enter the attic from there. It was worth a try, she decided.

Grabbing the chair, Sally smashed it against the windows. All the glass let go at once, and she was able to step outside onto the balcony without scratching herself. It was only then that she saw a doorway leading to the balcony. She hadn't needed to break the windows, after all. *Oh, well,* she thought. Cindy could pay for the damage.

Sally was out on the balcony studying the guard to see if it could support her weight when plaster and wood started raining down on her and she heard the wall above her being punched through. Turning, she was surprised to see Adam fly through the hole in the lighthouse and sail over the side.

Sally reached out and miraculously caught one of his arms. Adam hung over the side of the balcony, his feet dangling one hundred feet above the rocks.

"Adam!" she screamed, straining to hang on. "What are you doing?"

He looked up at her, his eyes wide as saucers.

"I thought I was about to die." He gasped. "Pull me up. Quick."

"I'm trying! You're so heavy."

"It's my high density, I know."

Somehow, Sally managed to pull Adam up far enough so he could place a foot on the floor of the balcony. From there he had no trouble climbing over the railing. Adam took a moment to catch his breath and get his bearings. During that time, Sally explained Watch's theory about Cindy's being related to the ghost. Actually, Sally took credit for making the connection. The news intrigued Adam. Sally also told him what Watch was up to. Adam nodded toward the hole in the lighthouse wall. The same hole the ghost had just thrown him out.

"We have to get back up inside there," he said. "The ghost will try to kill Cindy next."

"Cindy's a strong girl. She can take care of herself."

"Sally!"

"I was just kidding. Did you see any sign of Neil?"

"Yeah. He's in an attic above the attic. But help me balance on this railing. We don't have time to talk."

Sally steadied Adam as he climbed onto the railing. From there he had no trouble reaching the hole. The only problem was that Sally wasn't able to follow him. She had no one to help her balance on the railing.

"You'll have to talk to the ghost yourself," she called to Adam as he disappeared through the hole.

She stayed where she was, however, half expecting Adam to come flying out of the hole again. He was such a dynamic young man.

Inside the attic, Adam was met with a terrifying sight. The ghost had a hold of Cindy and was trying to drag her up the ladder to the second attic, probably to lock her inside with her brother. But Cindy was fighting back hard. She had a handful of the ghost's hair in her hand, and she was yanking on it, which the ghost obviously didn't like. Now the howling became bitter with pain and anger. Adam had to shout over it to be heard.

"Mrs. Makey!" he yelled. "You're holding Cindy Makey, your granddaughter!"

The ghost stopped and glanced over at him. So did Cindy.

"I'm not related to this ugly creature," Cindy swore.

Adam stepped forward. "What was your father's name?"

"I told you," Cindy said. "Frederick Makey. Why?"

Adam came even closer and spoke to the ghost. "What was the name of your son, Mrs. Makey?"

The ghost let go of Cindy and froze, staring at Adam. The fire in its eyes seemed to dim, and suddenly its face didn't look so scary. The light around it softened and took on a warmer yellow glow. The howling stopped as Adam spoke gently.

"Your son's name was Frederick Makey," he answered for the ghost. "The ghost of the ship that sank out on the reef did not steal your son. We have his skeleton below and you can talk to it if you like. He crashed his ship because he was drunk. Not because your light was off. It seems Rick just got washed out to sea. He must have washed ashore far from here, and was unable to get back home. But we know he didn't die that night thirty years ago because he later got married and had a family." Adam paused. "Honestly, Mrs. Makey, Cindy's your granddaughter."

The ghost turned back to Cindy. Gently it reached out to touch her hair. But doubt crossed its face and it stopped. Adam knew he had to act fast.

"Cindy," he said. "Tell Mrs. Makey something only your father and she could have known."

"I don't understand," Cindy mumbled, still standing on the stairs with the ghost only a foot away.

"It could be anything his mother taught him," Adam said. "Anything your father later taught you."

Cindy paused. "He taught me this poem. I know he knew it as a kid, but I don't know who taught it to him."

"Just say it," Adam snapped.
Cindy recited the poem quickly.

> The ocean is a lady.
> She is kind to all.
> But if you forget her dark moods.
> Her cold waves, those watery walls.
> Then you are bound to fall.
> Into a cold grave.
> Where the fish will have you for food.

> The ocean is a princess.
> She is always fair.
> But if you dive too deep.
> Into the abyss, the octopus's lair.
> Then you are bound to despair.
> In a cold grave.
> Where the sharks will have you for meat.

"It's sort of a lousy poem," Cindy said after she was finished.

"Please quit using the words *lousy* and *ugly* around Mrs. Makey," Adam said. The ghost's face became thoughtful. Adam asked softly, "Mrs. Makey, did you teach your son that poem?"

The ghost nodded slowly, and as it did a single tear

ran over its cheek. The tear did not appear to be made of water, however, but of diamond. It glistened in the glow cast by the powerful searchlight.

Once more the ghost turned back to Cindy. Adam understood what it needed to know. So did Cindy. She reached out to touch the ghost's shoulder.

"He was a great man, my father," Cindy whispered. "He had a happy life. He married a wonderful woman, and had us two kids." Then she lowered her head and there were tears on her face as well. "He died a couple of months ago, in a fire." Cindy sobbed. "I'm sorry. I know you miss him. I miss him, too."

The ghost did a remarkable thing right then. It hugged Cindy. No, it did more than that—it comforted her, and Cindy comforted it. For several seconds they cried in each other's arms, although Adam could not hear the ghost's tears.

Then the powerful light that poured through the floor dimmed.

Cindy and the ghost let go of each other.

Adam stepped forward. "Watch has sabotaged the generator. He's cut the power." Adam looked at the ghost. "I'm sorry. I don't know if this will hurt you. Our friend was just trying to save us."

To Adam's surprise, the ghost smiled and shook its head, as if to say that it was all right. Cindy got the same impression.

"I don't think she cares," Cindy said. "I think she wants to move on now." She grabbed the ghost's hands and spoke excitedly. "You can see my father! Your son!"

The ghost's smile widened. For the last time she hugged Cindy and nodded in Adam's direction. Almost as if to say thank you.

Then the searchlight failed and they were plunged into darkness.

At first it seemed completely dark. Then Adam noticed his flashlight lying on the floor. It was still on and he picked it up. After the searchlight the beam appeared feeble.

The ghost was gone.

Cindy quickly climbed the ladder to the top attic.

A moment later she reappeared with a five-year-old boy in her hands.

"Neil!" She was crying.

"Cindy!" her brother kept shouting happily. "Did you kill the ghost?"

"No," Adam said. "We just showed it the way home."

But their adventures were far from over.

All three of them smelled smoke.

Adam ran over to the door in the floor and opened it easily. But what he saw below did not reassure him. Far down, through the first trapdoor that led onto the steps, he saw huge orange flames on the ground floor of the lighthouse. Sally was in the room with the searchlight also looking down to the ground floor. Before Adam could speak, Watch poked his head through the floor at her feet. He had a big grin on his face.

"I was able to destroy the generator," he said.

"What did you do?" Sally screamed at him. "Blow it up?"

"As a matter of fact that is exactly what I did," Watch said, climbing into the room and standing beside Sally. He glanced back down at the flames, which were rapidly moving through the interior of the lighthouse. He lost his smile as he added, "It's too bad this place doesn't have a fire extinguisher."

"But we're trapped!" Sally screamed. "We're going to die!"

"I don't want to burn to death," Cindy whispered beside Adam, fear in her voice.

"We're not going to die," Adam said. "We've come too far for that to happen." He stood and spoke to all of them. "We're going to have to leap off the balcony and into the water."

"You're crazy," Sally said. "A hundred-foot fall will kill us."

"Not necessarily," Watch said. "It is the surface tension of the water that usually kills people when they jump from high places into water. But if that tension can be broken just before we hit the water, we should be all right."

"What does surface tension mean?" Neil asked his sister.

She rubbed his back. "I'll explain it later, after Watch explains it to me."

"Are you saying that if we have something like a board hit the water just before we do," Adam said, "we should live?"

"Exactly," Watch said. "Come down here. We'll break a few boards off the balcony railing."

Adam first helped Cindy and Neil down the ladder to join Watch and Sally and then climbed down himself. They hurried onto the balcony. A sharp cold wind had come up. It tore at their hair, while far below they could see huge waves crashing on the rocks. The surf had come up in the last few minutes.

It wasn't difficult to tear the railing apart to get all the boards they needed. Soon they each had a couple.

But they were quickly running out of time. Flames burst through to the searchlight room. The bulbs of the light fizzled and then exploded in a gruesome shower of glass and sparks. Orange light bathed the surroundings. The temperature soared.

"Do we throw them over the side ahead of us?" Sally asked.

"No," Watch said. "You'd never catch up with them. Throw the boards below you *after* you jump. They should hit the water a second before you."

"What if I hit to the side of my boards?" Sally asked.

"Then you'll die," Watch said.

There was nothing to say after that. There was no time to talk anyway. Fire licked out at them on the balcony. Smoke filled the air. It was almost impossible to breathe. They were all coughing. Together they drew back from the opening they had created in the railing. They needed a running start so they could fly beyond the rocks. Cindy held Neil in her arms, and wouldn't part with him, although Adam offered to take the boy. Adam realized he would have to throw Cindy's boards out for her.

They nodded at each other and then ran.

Over the side they flew.

It was the scariest thing imaginable.

For Adam it felt as if he fell forever. The cold wind ripped at his face and hair. He saw the waves, the rocks—all spun together. The ground seemed to take the place of the sky. He wasn't even sure which way was up and which way down. But he remembered to throw out his handful of boards.

Then there was an incredible smash.

Adam felt as if he had been crushed into a pancake.

Everything went cold and black.

He realized he was under the water. He couldn't see the others and for the moment he couldn't worry about them. He swam for the surface, hoping he was going in the right direction. A few seconds later his head broke into the night air. It felt wonderful to draw in a deep breath. He was the first one up. But the others appeared quickly, tiny heads peeking out of the rough surf.

"Can you swim?" he shouted at Neil.

"I'm a great swimmer," the boy said proudly.

They swam to the end of the jetty, where they had earlier tied the rope. They had to time getting onto the rocks, so they didn't get crushed by waves. But the night was finally kind. There was a sudden lull in the waves and soon they were on dry land. Or at least on a bunch of rocks that they could walk on to dry land.

Cindy was so excited to see her brother. She refused to let go of Neil, hugging him and burying him with kisses. Adam was happy for both of them.

"Your mom will be surprised to see your brother again," he told Cindy.

"That's putting it mildly," Cindy said. "Oh, I want you to meet my mother. She likes to meet all the guys I hang out with."

"It's not clear yet whether you and Adam will be having an ongoing relationship," Sally said.

Cindy chuckled. "I think we're all going to be friends. Even you and me, Sally."

"We'll see," Sally said, doubtful. But then she smiled and patted Watch and Adam on the back. "Another heroic mission successfully concluded. I must say you guys did a good job."

"You were the one who figured out the secret of the mystery," Adam said. "Without you, the ghost would have killed us all."

"What's this?" Watch asked.

"Nothing," Sally said quickly. "I'll explain it to you later." She pointed out to sea. "It's amazing we never saw any sharks today. I guess these waters aren't as dangerous as I thought."

But Sally spoke too soon.

A huge white fin sailed by just then.

They jumped up on the biggest rock and grabbed on to one another.

"You must never forget where we live," Adam whispered.

"Ain't that the truth," Sally said, gasping.

On the way home they stopped for doughnuts. Except for Neil, they all ordered coffee. They needed to settle their nerves. The day had been a little too exciting.

About the Author

Little is known about Christopher Pike, although he is supposed to be a strange man. It is rumored that he was born in New York but grew up in Los Angeles. He has been seen in Santa Barbara lately, so he probably lives there now. But no one really knows what he looks like, or how old he is. It is possible that he is not a real person, but an eccentric creature visiting from another world. When he is not writing, he sits and stares at the walls of his huge haunted house. A short, ugly troll wanders around him in the dark and whispers scary stories in his ear.

Christopher Pike is one of this planet's best-selling authors of young adult fiction.

LOOK FOR

Christopher Pike's

SPOOKSVILLE™ #3

THE HAUNTED CAVE

COMING MID-NOVEMBER 1995

Don't miss any of the adventure!

Whenever pets–and their owners–get into trouble, Rosie Saunders and Kayo Benton always seem to be in the middle of the action. Ever since they started the Care Club ("We Care About Animals"), they've discovered a world of mysteries and surprises. . .and danger!

#1: CAT BURGLAR ON THE PROWL
#2: BONE BREATH AND THE VANDALS
#3: DON'T GO NEAR MRS. TALLIE
#4: DESERT DANGER

By Peg Kehret

A MINSTREL® BOOK

Published by Pocket Books

1049-04

Are You Afraid of the Dark? ™

A brand new thriller series based on the hit

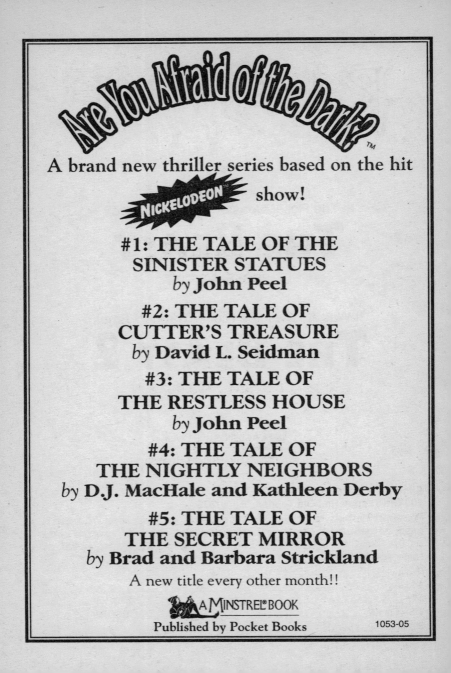 show!

A new title every other month!!

A MINSTREL® BOOK
Published by Pocket Books

1053-05